The First Time

REVISITED

The First Time
REVISITED

5-Stories of first erotic Ménage à trois

A Black Widow Collection
Featuring V.B.Eghan

Passionate Books for Passionate People

PO Box 51911
Ft Myers, FL 33994
www.BlackWidowPublishing.com

Black Widow Books

The First Time Revisited
5-Stories of first erotic Ménage à trois

Black Widow Books may be ordered through booksellers or by contacting:

Black Widow Publishing, LLC
PO Box 51911
Fort Myers, FL 33994
www.BlackWidowPublishing.com
(904) BWP-8469 (904-297-8469)

ISBN: 978-1-943322-02-2 (Print)
ISBN: 978-1-943322-03-9 (Digital)

Printed in the United States of America

Editor: Susan Allen
Cover designs & book design: Jennifer FitzGerald - www.MotherSpider.com

Any people depicted in stock imagery are models, and such images are being used for illustrative purposes only. Images copyright: 123rf.com and dollarphotoclub.com

WARNING: Due to the sexual content within this book it is not suitable for those under 18. This book contains adult themes which some readers may find objectionable and/or offensive, including graphic depictions of sexual intercourse. Please do not read if you find the above subject matter to be offensive. We support those under 18 experiencing life slowly and ask that you wait until you have lived what is considered 'normal' for a while first, before reading literary works such as these.

From the Publisher

Welcome to a Black Widow Collection. We publish a lot of shorter, ebook stories that are not long enough for print, although we know you are one who enjoys holding a good book in hand. For that reason, we release most of our shorts in collections as well.

Please take the time to visit our website and meet all the authors you are about to enjoy. Then, join our Reader's Club and get 50% off all our printed books. Each month we feature one of our authors and you can join us on a live webinar to ask questions and get to know them more.

See you on the inside!

http://BlackWidowPublishing.com

Table of Contents

A BIRTHDAY SURPRISE!

NUDISTS, SWINGERS, SEX CLUBS...OH MY!

Black Widow Books

BIRTHDAY GIRL GETS AND EYE OPENING
EXPERIENCE AND MORE WHEN THIER HOTEL IS
NOT WHAT THAN THEY EXPECTED

V.B.EGHAN

A Birthday Surprise

Vanessa Breck Eghan

In a perfect world, no one would ever have to second guess themselves about anything. Your choices would all be correct. Your words would be good ones. There would be no aftermath of uncertainty, in anything you did. The world is not perfect however, and mine seems even less so, most of the time. The year of my fortieth birthday shifted my life into so many different directions. Some of them turned out good, even excellent. Some not so much, but all of them led me to the point I am at now, so I accept each twist and turn as part of my overall growing experience.

My husband, Paul decided to take me on a surprise trip for my birthday. It was a milestone year, and he wanted to do something really special for me. I had recently lost a considerable amount of weight and had gotten myself into great shape. He liked showing his new 'trophy wife' off. In truth, we are childhood sweethearts. We'd been together 25 years by then, married for 22. We have literally grown up together. He is my rock, my partner, and the love of my life. I wasn't always sure he had the same depth of emotion for me, but about the time I was pregnant with our second child, things changed. That is all fodder for another story. Back to my birthday surprise.

Paul really went all out, something he had never done before. He took me shopping a few days before my actual birthday. He had me pick out and try on so many new sexy clothes. They were all revealing in one way or another. Plunging necklines, no backs, sheer, short, you get the picture.

I got new shoes for each outfit. He picked out lingerie for me. He even bought a few Brazilian style bikinis. I hadn't been able to entertain the idea of a bikini since high school. Diet and exercise had finally paid off for me, and I looked damned good! Even if I do say so myself.

We live in Florida, so I guessed by the clothing, we were going to stay in a warm climate. I picked out lots of different jewelry to bring with me. I have worked in a professional position for many years, and have built up an impressive assortment of costume jewelry to wear with my work clothes. I threw in a couple pairs of cut off shorts, tank tops, and sun dresses for good measure. Paul isn't usually a stylish dresser himself, I had my doubts about him picking all my clothes. Everything was beautiful and sexy, yet as far as I knew, we could be heading for Disney World.

Finally, the day came for us to head out on our adventure. Paul had taken Thursday through Monday off from work. He had arranged for me to be off as well. My boss was happy to oblige, since I rarely take time off. We packed our suitcases into the car, and headed south from where we lived. I tried to guess where we were going, but everything I came up with was wrong. Paul and I talked, laughed, and sang along with the radio. We had been driving for over an hour before we made our first stop. It was the last exit available to buy gas for fifty miles, before heading across Alligator Alley toward the east coast. Paul filled up the gas tank while I went inside to get us some drinks.

I had dressed 'surfer casual' in a white eyelet, mid-thigh length skirt, with a silky, chocolate brown tank top. I cinched my waist with a cool, O'Neil fabric belt, with gold and white squiggles on a darker brown background, and a big round wooden buckle. My suede flip flops were the same shade of brown as the shirt, with tiny seashells sewed onto the thong part. I let my waist-length blonde hair air dry, so it had that 'just hopped out of bed', sexy, loose curl to it. I had only put a touch of makeup on that day, some mascara, and light pink lip stain. My green eyes stood out with less makeup. The tan I always sported was intentionally deeper golden than usual. I had been lying naked by our pool, at least an hour, every day for months. I didn't know where we were going, but I wanted to look like a star when we got there. What I achieved was a 'California girl' look. Not quite the movie star I was going for. Paul loved the look, so I was happy.

While I was in the store, a young Hispanic man whistled at me, as I walked by, and asked me where I was going. That made me ecstatic. I felt sexy as I sauntered back to the car, with a little more swing in my walk than normal. Paul watched me as I came back.

When I got in the car, he asked, "Who are your friends?"

"Um, what? Who?" I turned back and saw the Hispanic man and a couple friends were outside the shop leaning against the wall. They were undaunted by Paul's presence, and even started blowing kisses at me. I giggled. "I guess they liked what they saw. One of them whistled at me in the store."

"Well, who wouldn't like looking at you?" Paul flattered me.

We didn't stay on Alligator Alley long. We

exited and headed down state road twenty-nine, then east on Forty One. The scenic route. I love to take the scenic route almost anywhere. We stopped at a Miccosukee Indian Village and had lunch. I ordered gator bites, I fell in love with them the first time I ever visited Florida. Now that I live here, I order them whenever I see them on the menu. Paul is not the daring eater that I am, so he stuck to a burger. We ate side by side in our booth. We kissed and held hands more than usual. It was a perfect day so far. We were the picture of happiness. I am sure we looked to strangers like we were newly in love.

We finally got to our destination, which I still had no idea about. It was a five-story build-ing on the A1A, one block from the beach. As we pulled in, I saw what looked like a Tiki bar on the roof. Awesome! I was ready to party. I also noticed the name on the small sign hanging in front of the building; Pool-Top Resort. Hmm… It didn't look like a resort from the outside. In fact, it looked run down and very old Florida hotel-ish. My happy was starting to fade. We pulled into a parking spot. Paul hopped out, grabbed a luggage cart, and loaded it up. I stepped out of the car and looked around. I was not impressed, but I wasn't about to show it. I was determined to make the best of this.

We entered the small lobby which was quite

run down. A man behind the counter, which dominated the room, looked up over his reader glasses, and asked how he could help us. He and Paul finished the check in process. The man handed Paul a second set of keys and said, "Those are for the side door. All doors downstairs need to remain locked at all times after six P.M., only guests can come and go using the side entrance." Weird.

We rolled our luggage rack over to the elevator doors and pushed the button. It was taking a relatively long time to come down from the fifth floor. Our room was on the second floor. If it hadn't been for our luggage, we would have just walked, but we decided to wait it out.

The elevator light finally showed it was on the first floor. With a 'ding' the doors opened. I was not expecting what my eyes beheld. There was a rather tall, barrel bellied, furry chested, man holding a beer in one hand, and a cooler in the other. He started to step off the elevator, realized he was on the first floor and stepped right back in. He used the arm with the cooler to block the door from closing, and motioned with his head for us to come in. He was absolutely buck naked. You don't see that every day.

Paul and I were raised during the sixties and seventies. Although we missed the boat on being actual 'I was at Woodstock' hippies. We still had that kind of lifestyle and attitude, for the most part. Once our children left the house, we became card-carrying nudists. We actually joined a couple clubs that owned private beach property, and lakefront properties. Barbecues and sunbathing were the extent of the activities we had participated in. So we politely averted our eyes from the large man's tiny penis and got into the elevator. Paul maneuvered the luggage cart so it was a barrier between us and 'naked guy'. I looked at all the ads on the wall of the elevator. They were for erotic massage, couples massage, bus service to a club I had never heard of; Trapeze, and a lingerie store with adult toys on the fourth floor of the hotel. I was beginning to see the full picture here.

The elevator stopped at the second floor and we quickly got out. Naked guy waved and said, "See ya'll at the pool."

We turned from the elevator, and took in the view on the second floor. It was a big open court-yard with live palm trees and a huge fountain. The rooms ran up either side of the open courtyard from the elevator. The far wall parallel to the elevator was a bar. There was a small café style bistro table with two chairs, made of wrought iron, outside each room. The wall perpendicular to the elevator had a long plush red velvet settee with gold painted ornate wood. There were faux leopard pillows with black fringe at each arm. It was something straight out of an interior designer's nightmare. The look on Paul's face was priceless. He looked mortified. I know he was afraid I would hate it, and I sort of did. It didn't look very clean. My family jokes that I have OCD about cleanliness. Maybe I do a little. I wasn't about to be a spoilsport and ruin Paul's surprise. He had worked so hard to make this nice for me. Besides, I was in such a good mood, I wanted it to continue.

"Where is our room?" I asked in almost a whisper. I don't know why I was so quiet. There was not a single soul around.

"230," Paul said, scouring the courtyard trying to see what the number sequence was. He pointed to our right at the first door. We headed that way.

There was a large picture window that opened up to the courtyard area. There was also an inflatable hot tub almost directly outside of it. Gross! There was a pump on the hot tub, and it was running as we got closer. I realized it would definitely drive me crazy the second I heard how loud it was. Why was it parked outside our window? I supposed it was the only corner left to stuff one more 'tacky' thing into. I was so wrong.

It took several tries to get the key to unlock the door. It was an actual key, but it was old and the tumblers were probably rusted. We opened the room and it was actually, sort of a suite.

There was a full kitchen off the main room

which had a king size bed. There was a small sitting room also off the main sleeping area. It had a TV, a sofa bed, and some weird free standing air conditioner unit with ducts running to the window. The closet door was off its track and lying in the closet up at its top. The hot water heater was located in the other half of the closet so there was only half the usable space. The bathroom was disgusting. It was dirty, moldy, hairy, and old, old, old. The tiles were all cracked and stained. The shower curtain was moldy, the walls were a veritable petri dish of excrements. There was no stopper in the tub, it was horribly stained by rust. (I hoped)

Paul looked around, then looked at me with very sad eyes. "It sounded so beautiful and looked really nice on the web-site. I am so sorry, baby."

"Let's go take a look around. We can go to the store later, and get some cleaning stuff. I will call the desk for a new shower curtain, and sink and tub stoppers. Besides I'm thirsty. I need a beer." I couldn't let his obvious disappointment set in.

"Good plan." Paul looked relieved that I wasn't throwing a hissy fit and demanding we go someplace else.

"Just tell me, what possessed you to book a trip here?" I was curious.

"Well, the web-site said it was a clothing optional resort. The pictures looked great, and it was so close to the beach. I got us tickets to a comedy show at the Hard Rock. It isn't too far from here. I figured nude pool and sunbathing, and a great place to stay. Holy shit was I wrong. I am so sorry." He reiterated his apology.

"Stop saying you are sorry. You couldn't have known. But tell me, did you know it was a swingers place? I was sure he hadn't figured it out yet.

"A what?!"

"Swingers Club. Couldn't you tell by the posters on the wall in the elevator?"

"No. Really? A swingers club? How do you know?" He was mystified.

"I'm telling you, the posters, the set-up, naked guy inviting us to the pool, it all screams swinger lifestyle." I am sure the smugness in my voice was noticed.

"What do you mean when you say 'lifestyle'?" He wanted to know.

"Well, that's what swingers call it. They say they are in the 'lifestyle.'"

"Oh, that makes sense. The web-site said lifestyle friendly…Wait how did you know that? He sounded concerned.

"I read. Some of my books are pretty smutty. Why do you think I get so horny when we are on vacation? It's all those trashy novels I bring with me. Sometimes they are about swingers." That was true. "Let's go get a drink and check this place out. I'm curious now."

A Birthday Surprise

I was eager to see what other people were here. Not that I wanted to try swinging. I just wanted to see what kind of people did.

"OK, after you then. He held the door open for me. His smile was sexy. I was happy he was smiling again.

The first thing we did was make a complete circuit of the second floor. We walked across the floor to the room directly facing ours. The curtains were pulled back and what was inside was no ordinary room. There was a black faux leather covered mattress right inside the window on the floor. Past that, more toward the middle of the room, was a sex swing. 'Interesting.' There were flat wooden benches along the walls and a small wardrobe type cabinet with nicely rolled up towels in it. There was a TV mounted in one corner of the room, it was playing porn on a loop. Some really perky blonde, with bright red lips, was on her knees deep-throating a very well hung stud. He had one hand on his hip and the other holding the back of her head, forcing her deeper until she gagged. We watched for a minute or two and moved on. I could feel the wetness between my legs as we walked. Porn turns me on. What can I say?

The next room also had its curtains drawn back. There was a large round, red leather bed in the center. The ceiling and one entire wall were mirrored. There was a sofa against the wall. It was black leather. It was warped, and cracking from lack of care and age. In the far corner of the room was a chair which resembled a giant woman's high heeled shoe. The shoe was covered in faux zebra plush, with a felt red underside to resemble a Louboutin I supposed. Behind the shoe chair was a floor lamp with a gold boudoir shade with black fringe hanging from the bottom. Another TV was mounted in similar fashion, and it too was on a porn loop. This time, the movie was Gay porn. Two extremely attractive young hairless men were doing it doggy style. The guy who was receiving was taking it like a champ. The giver was pounding the hell out of him. They both seemed to be enjoying it. Paul was uncomfortable, so we moved on. I became wetter still.

Room three was a regular looking hotel room with two queen size beds side-by-side and a cheap looking nightstand between them. There was a woman in the room unpacking a suitcase. She was overweight for her height by about fifty pounds. She looked to be in her mid to late fifties. Her hair was jet black and very thick, it was all one length and hung to her shoulders. She was naked except for a sarong, which she wrapped around her hips and tied off to one side. It was short. Too short. I could easily see she had no pubic hair. Her exposed breasts were enormous sagging almost all the way to her waist. She had huge dark areolas, a sure sign she had had children, her nipples pointed at her toes. She saw us looking in as we walked by. She smiled and waved mid-fold of something she pulled out of her case.

I could see that the bathroom door was wide open and there was a completely naked man brushing his teeth. He was tall, over six foot. He had a beer gut but not as large as naked elevator guy. He had a full head of wavy gray hair. I assumed he was slightly older than the woman he was with. He also waved, smiling at us, and revealed, even with a toothbrush in his mouth, the most crooked yellow teeth I had ever seen. Yuck! His penis was unbelievably tiny. I had never seen one so small on a grown man. It looked like just balls and a dick head. How sad. As we passed the open door to their room, we waved and moved on.

The rest of the rooms all had the shades drawn. I assumed they were occupied, but the place was empty. So was the bar. No patrons, no bartender. Paul and I got back on the elevator, and pushed the button for the third floor. All the rooms were just regular rooms, as far as we could tell, on the third floor. Most had the curtains open looking unoccupied.

The fourth floor was the same mostly unoccupied. The Adult Toy/lingerie store was closed. The window display showed an array of sex toys, and some negligees and panties. I made a mental note to find out the hours, as they were not posted.

The fifth floor also seemed to be mostly unoccupied. On the same back wall as the bar was on the second level, were two rooms with no windows at all. They were numbered in sequence with the other rooms, so I assumed they were guest rooms. As we made the turn around the rail heading back to the elevator, the second room on that wall had a light on and the curtains were partly drawn. They were open enough to see a middle aged bald guy lying on the bed jerking himself off. We rushed past that one. He had left his door wide open.

We took the elevator up one more story and it opened to the roof. To our left was a large rectangular pool. To our right was a huge rooftop patio with cheap looking, white plastic, chaise lounges lined up along the roofs railing, two rows deep. As we stepped out of the entryway, to our immediate right was a smallish Tiki bar. It had a thatched roof with small Christmas lights strung around the inside. There was a twenty-something man with thick blond hair and thick bookworm type glasses behind the bar. (Think John Denver) There was a naked couple in the pool at the opposite end from us. The woman was sitting on the steps in the water facing us, and the man had his back to us. They both looked our way momentarily, then went back to their own discussion.

We decided we would go out to find some dinner and a beer, then come back and hang out up here on the roof. It was only Thursday night. Most parties happened on the weekend, right?

It was a one block walk to the beach so we headed that way. Right on the corner there was a bar and grill. It was open to the beach and the view was beautiful. We found seats at the bar. We ordered beer and burgers. The food was good, but the beer was better. They were playing music over the sound system. It was an eclectic mix of classic rock and pop music. The beer and the atmosphere were working their magic on me. I was singing and bopping in my chair. I love the beach. It has a magical effect on me. I am one of those people who feels totally calm and relaxed by the sea. After we had eaten, we decided to go and get this night started. We made a quick pit stop at a convenience store just a short walk from the bar. I bought a broom and dustpan and several cleaning supplies. We also picked up a twelve pack of Corona and lime. Supplies in tow, we headed back to the hotel.

We stopped in the lobby where I told the manager how disgusted I was at the condition of the room. He told me he would send someone up with a new shower curtain, and he could have housekeeping come back if I wanted. He wasn't exactly apologetic, and I got the feeling he really didn't care.

I turned down the housekeeping. I wasn't ready to piss them off on the first day of our stay. I had already made the desk clerk unhappy.

Back in the room I swept, and scrubbed every inch. I shook out the bed sheets, and pulled the threadbare comforter completely off. I plugged an air freshener in the bathroom outlet, and left bleach on all the moldy areas to soak. I was finally comfortable enough to unpack.

Once that task was accomplished, we got undressed. I wrapped a sarong crisscrossed over my breasts and tied it behind my neck. Paul opted to wear a bathing suit at least until we got up to the pool area. Satisfied with our attire, we left the room, and headed for the elevator. I noticed a layer of oily scum on top of the water in the blow up hot tub, as we walked by. I visibly shuddered as I imagined what might be its source.

Back up at the pool area we headed straight for the bar. The young blonde was still there. It was a little after seven by now. There was a different, forty-something couple in the pool relaxing. They were nude. I sat on a towel, on a barstool, and asked for a beer. The bartender explained they didn't actually serve alcohol, they served you back your own drinks in plastic cups, and they provided some mixers, and soft drinks. What? I had never heard of that before. So Paul headed back to our room to bring up our twelve pack and lime.

The bar tender's name was Nate. He was happily bisexual, and had a treasure chest of 'toys' he was proud of. He showed them to me in the first five minutes of our conversation. I didn't actually 'get it' at that moment, but he was trying to see if I would be interested in having sex with him. Paul came back with our drinks, and Nate happily cut up the lime, and served us back our own beers. He let us keep the bottles but made us promised not to leave the bar with them. We all settled into a pleasant conversation about the weather and the view.

The sun was beginning its descent in the west. The colors of the eastern sky were becoming more and more vivid. Oranges and pinks swirled with blues, greens, and purple. The breeze had picked up, and was blowing the warm salt air over us. The radio at the bar was tuned to a pop station that was playing decent music. Between conversations I, of course, was singing along. I love to sing. I may not be very good, but I can carry a tune. Mostly it just makes me feel good.

Paul was being the ultimate gentleman. He stood up when I excused myself to the restroom, and held my chair when I sat back down. He made sure I didn't ever want for a cold beer. As soon as I finished one, he motioned to Nate to bring me another. It wasn't long before I was really feeling the effects.

We decided it was time to take a dip in the pool. We walked to the water's edge and I kicked off a flip flop and dipped my toe in. The couple in the pool acknowledged us as we stood there.

"Hi," said the woman. She was average build, had mousy brown short hair, and a sweet smile.

"Hello. How are you?" Paul asked politely.

"What's up?" Her man, a muscle bound, balding, heavily tattooed gentleman responded.

Paul and I continued to disrobe the few garments we had on, and got in the pool. We both ducked under, and swam across, then back. We were pretty close to the other couple so we introduced ourselves.

Their names were Joe and Heidi. We spent a few minutes socializing with them while relaxing in the warm water. We talked about the weather and how quiet it was at the hotel. Joe said it probably would be busier over the weekend. They told us they had been coming there for years. After what might have been half an hour, they both climbed out of the pool.

"I hope it's nothing we did." Paul joked.

"No, man we are going to the place across the street for dinner. We'll be back."

We all laughed, and they gathered their belongings and headed for the elevator, naked except for their flip flops. The sky had darkened considerably. The pool lights came on. It gave a beautiful blue glow to the night around us. I swam up on Paul's lap, wrapped my legs around his hips, and we began to kiss. As the kiss deepened, I felt that familiar tingle between my legs.

"There is no sex in the pool. Read the sign." The bartender Nate had come over from the bar. He motioned with his head to a dilapidated sign on the rail near the pool.

"Well that is okay, we didn't think there was." Paul sassed. He was apparently pissed off that anyone would assume we were having sex in the pool.

Obviously shaken by Paul's defensive posture, Nate backpedaled quickly. "Nothing personal, we have to tell everyone who looks like they might be getting into it. Can I bring you guys a beer?"

"Sure," I said before Paul had a chance to answer. The tension needed to be broken.

Paul and I read the pool rules sign as Nate went to fetch our drinks. Rule 1- No diving. Rule 2 – No glass in or around the pool. Rule 3 – No running. Rule 4 – If you are having diarrhea do not use the pool. Oh my god! Well, that made us laugh, but it also made us both a little sick at the thought. Rule 5 – No sexual activity in the pool or surrounding areas. So, there it was, in writing. What a bizarre set of rules. This place was getting stranger by the moment.

The First Time

Nate returned with our beers poured into a red plastic cup. He hung around the edge of the pool making small talk when he finally blurted out "You two up for some fun tonight?"

"Not right now," Paul stated. "We are just going to relax and have a few drinks."

"Well, my shift is over, so I will just leave your beer behind the bar. Help yourself. You sure you don't want to play?" Nate sounded almost desperate.

"We are sure. Thanks though," Paul was doing all the talking, and I was glad. I didn't know how to handle this situation.

"Alright, but if you change your mind, I will be around for a while."

"Well, thanks," Paul said with a hint of sarcasm. Then looked at me with his brows arched in a question.

Nate left and I felt relieved. Things felt so awkward there for a little while. That man was odd. This place was strange. I shook it off and swam around the pool a little. I came back over to Paul, grabbed my cup from the side of the pool, and took a huge gulp of my beer. Maybe it was my drunken state that made everything seem so off? I could tell Paul felt it too. He had become quiet.

"What's the matter baby?" I had to ask.

"I swear, I had no idea what kind of place this was. If you want to, we can leave."

His sincerity moved me. "I'm fine babe. Really. We can stay."

"I just don't want you to think I planned this to try to get you to do something."

"I know. Seriously, it is okay."

"Are you sure? This place is kind of creepy."

"I'm sure. Let's just have fun ourselves, and not think too much about what is going on around us."

We climbed out of the pool, toweled off, and dressed. We walked to the railing and admired the view of the Caribbean blue water, and the white sand. They were ablaze with the colors of the sunset, even though the sunset was on the opposite side of the water. We could hear music from a live band drifting up from somewhere below us. It was mostly Salsa and dance.

Paul moved behind me and nestled himself up against my back. He started kissing my neck, and my earlobes. That always makes my eyes roll back in my head, and my toes curl. The heat between my legs was intensifying. I could feel Paul's erection pushing against the small of my back.

I turned to face him and we kissed. Deep and hot. Our tongues fought for control. I could taste the beer on our breath. Paul reached up with one hand and began fondling my breasts. He used the other hand to steady himself, and ground his crotch into mine.

The First Time

"I think we are breaking rule number 5," I whispered. "Let's take this party to our room."

"You read my mind. Let's go."

We grabbed the two beers we had left behind the bar, and put our already cut lime into one of the plastic cups. We got on the elevator and went back to our room.

Inside the room, we pulled each other's clothes off, and practically dove onto the bed. I was incredibly horny. Paul's erection let me know he was as well. We kissed, and petted, and groped at each other, rolling around on the bed. Paul reached his hand down to feel my very wet pussy. He slid a finger into my slit and began to pump in and out. I purred and moaned softly at the delicious intrusion.

Another finger joined the first and his thumb began to rub my clitoris. I was sighing, and rocking to the rhythm of his fingers, when he pulled his hand away. My sharp intake of breath told of my disappointment at the sudden loss. Paul maneuvered himself down the bed until he was standing at the foot. He hooked his arms under my thighs and pulled me down so my behind was right at the bottom edge. He dropped to his knees and immediately stuffed his face right into my v.

Paul is a master at reading my body, and this was just what I wanted. He began to lick and swirl his tongue around my clit and my slit, lapping at my free flowing juices. I could feel an orgasm starting to build deep in my core. The familiar tingle drove me to push his head hard onto me.

Knowing I was close to going over the edge, Paul added fingers to his ministrations. First one, then two fingers pumped at my g-spot as he sucked my clit. It wasn't long until I was there.

"Oh god, I am going to cum baby!" I cried out just as the spasms of orgasm overtook me. My mind and body exploded into millions of sparks of pleasure. I thrust my hips into his face, and held his head to me with both hands. Paul removed his fingers and replaced them with his tongue. He slurped hungrily at the slick wetness escaping me. I screamed out in pleasure.

"Yes! Yes! Yes! Right there baby! Don't stop!" He didn't.

I am luckily multi-orgasmic, which Paul is well aware of. He slowed his pace, eventually stopping the sweet torture between my legs. He stood back up, hefted my thighs off the bed in the crook of his arms, and slammed his cock into me. I immediately began to climax again.

My cries were now unintelligible. I was panting rapidly. Paul pumped ferociously into me while continuing to hold my legs in the air. I couldn't do anything but take his pound-ing. After a few minutes of this, and my almost constant state of cumming, I could tell that Paul too, was ready to go over the edge. He growled and grunted animal like.

"I'm going to cum babe, here I cum!" He shouted out as his orgasm hit him. "Aghhhh!!!" And with a couple final pumps, I felt his semen mingle with my juices. He collapsed on top of me, freeing my legs, yet keeping himself buried inside me.

It took a few minutes for our breathing to stabilize. I got up to go clean myself up. When I came out of the bathroom, Paul had pulled himself up to the pillows, and was softly snoring. I shook my head as I thought 'men.'

I busied myself with cleaning the room up some more, rinsing all the areas of bleach I had left soaking in the bathroom and kitchen. Once I was finished, I climbed on the bed next to Paul, and fell asleep myself.

Our cat-nap was short lived. Voices and noise, outside our door, stirred us. I peeked out the curtain. I was shocked to see Nate, the couple that was unpacking, and the first couple from the pool all sitting in the hot tub. They were all naked, and in various sexual acts right there in the hot tub.

Nate was in between the two women, sucking one of the dark haired woman's enormous breasts, while fondling the other woman's tits with a free hand. The other two men were on the opposite sides of the women, although not the women they had arrived with. The tall gray haired man had his hands in the water in a position I was sure led to the younger woman's privates. The younger man was playing with the dark haired woman's unsuckled breast. It was a sight. I motioned for Paul to come over and put a finger to my lips to shush him before he said anything.

I could see the shock on Paul's face as he took in the scene unfolding before him. He turned back and looked at me. "I guess there is no doubt you were right anymore."

"Of course I was right. I am always right," I joked.

We peeked out the curtain together, voyeurs watching the real life porn in front of us. The final scene played out befor our eyes. Nate was fucking the dark haired woman from behind as she leaned over the edge of the hot tub with her boobs hanging nearly to the floor outside the tub. The younger woman was deep throating her man while jacking off the tiny dicked older man. Both men were standing, and she appeared to be on her knees.

The gross part of all this happened when they began to cum. Nate pulled his long skinny dick out of the dark haired woman, and splooged all over her giant ass. Tiny dicked man and younger guy both spurted onto the face and tongue of the younger woman. All of them sat back down in the small hot tub and rinsed the jizz off right in the water. Eeeewww!!!! One by one, they got up, kissed each other, and then stepped out of the hot tub, and walked away. I don't think I had ever been so grossed out over anything before.

"That is disgusting!" I said to Paul.

"Note to self, say no to the hot tub," He joked.

Once the group moved far enough away, Paul pulled our curtain open. I dressed in a white, see-through, backless dress. I wore no under-garments. I put on some strappy gold heels, and lots of gold jewelry: a thick gold chain around my neck, large gold hoops in my ears, and mul-tiple gold bangles on both arms. My nails were done French style, clear with white tips. My 8 carat, cushion cut diamond, set in gold, gleamed next to my wedding band with small channel set diamonds. These were not my original engage-ment and wedding rings. They were a 25th anni-versary gift from Paul. I loved them. I touched up my minimal makeup, but this time I added a little blush to my cheekbones. Using a dollop of mousse, I tossed my hair giving it that sleep mussed look.

Paul dressed in black linen pants, and a white gauze, pullover, short sleeved, beach shirt with a deep V-neck, which showed off his chest and biceps nicely. He wore a gold chain I bought him, around his neck, and a pair of casual loafers. Paul is purposely bald. He began shaving his head in the military for the ease of it, and just never stopped. He sported a goatee, and the overall look oozed sex.

We exited the hotel in search of more beer. It was a short walk to the convenience store at the corner. This time we bought three twelve packs and three more limes. I carried one twelve pack and the limes, while Paul took the other two twelve packs. We headed back to our room.

When we reached the second floor, we were surprised to see people milling about. There was a bartender at the second floor bar. He was a small, Hispanic looking man, with nice eyes and a friendly smile. He waved across the floor at us. We waved back and disappeared into our room. Paul put the limes and beer in the fridge except for two. He pulled the tops on them, and added two of the already cut limes to their rim. I watched him as he did this. God he is so sexy to me! How I love this man. I must have been grinning as he walked toward me.

"What?" He said, his eyebrows arching quizzically.

"Oh nothing, I was just thinking about how lucky I am," I told him.

"Yeah, yeah what can I say," he answered. He

handed me a beer and leaned in for a deep, long kiss. We broke the kiss smiling at each other and walked outside.

We took a seat on the patio set outside our door. Thankfully it was on the opposite side of the door from the hot tub. I wouldn't have been able to stomach that. Within minutes of us sitting, the bartender came over to our table with two plastic wine glasses and a bottle of wine. He said it was compliments of the hotel for new guests. Well at least they did something right here, I thought. I watched as he poured the red wine into the plastic and I asked him his name.

"I am Manuel," he said proudly in a thick accent. "If you need anything, I will be at the bar until one a.m. I can put your beer over there, and serve them to you if you wish."

Paul put his hands up and said "No thanks. We'll just keep them in our fridge. Thanks for the wine."

"I will put the rest behind the bar for you. If you need more, just call Manuel, and I will bring it." With that, he walked back to the bar. There was a couple I had not seen before sitting at the bar. Manuel went right to work serving them back their own drinks.

As we sat outside our door, we drank and talked, and laughed. Couples emerged from their rooms. Some stayed near the bar, some sat at the patio tables. They came and went.

Manuel came back and poured us more of our wine. Paul gave me his. He is not much of a wine drinker. I am, but this wine was pretty bad. I drank it anyway. Manuel left some bar snacks in plastic cups on our table at one point. Some kind of off-brand pretzel mix, and peanuts. We munched on them absentmindedly as we sipped our beer.

Some time after midnight, we noticed it was just us and Manuel left on the second floor. Had everyone gone to bed, or out to clubs? I didn't notice which way they had gone.

"I guess the party is over," Paul remarked.

"Where do you think everyone went?" I wondered.

"No idea. What do you want to do?"

"I am fine right here." I was more than fine, I was very drunk. "I don't think I am stable enough to go anywhere right now."

"Oh yeah? Does that mean I am going to get to take advantage of you?" Paul was always thinking about sex. I usually was too. We were really a perfect couple.

Just then, a perfect looking couple stepped off the elevator. He was tall and swarthy with a head full of black wavy hair. She was very tall. Her shapely legs went on forever. She had a tiny waist yet was curvy in all the right places.

The First Time

Her light brown hair was swept up in a messy up-do. Errant hairs framed her face. They were both dressed as if they had just come from a dance club. Her dress reminded me of that white number that gets blown up by the passing subway that you see Marilyn Monroe in, except it was much shorter. He was in all black. His partially unbuttoned shirt revealed a lot of dark chest hair. He was carrying a duffle bag.

They went into the room directly across from ours. The one which had the swing and leather mattress. Paul and I sat up a little strainer in our chairs and watched through the open window. He set the bag down on the bed and she opened it and pulled out a sheet. A sheet? Who brings a sheet to a hotel? She spread it out over the leather mattress. Then she pulled two large towels out of the bag and rolled one up, but spread the other on top of the sheet. By now they noticed we were watching. They both smiled in our direction but went right back to setting up the room.

Manuel came over with more snacks. "I leave now," he said. "Enjoy the show." He motioned with his head to the room the couple was in.

"Thank you, Manuel. Will we see you tomorrow?" I asked.

"I be at the pool tomorrow." He said and smiled a gleaming white, toothy, smile that showed to his eyes. "Good night."

A Birthday Surprise

"Good night," Paul and I said in unison. As soon as Manuel walked away, we turned our attention back to the play room.

Oh, the things that can happen in the blink of an eye. The lovely couple was now naked, and lovely they truly were. Her tits were perfect. Her ass was well rounded and tight enough to bounce a quarter off. Her legs looked even longer if that were possible. Her stomach was flat and had a small six pack. Her graceful arms were just muscular enough to show she worked out without being obnoxious. She was totally clean shaven and sleek from her neck down. Her skin was evenly pale all over. No tan lines anywhere. He however, was tan all over, with bulging biceps and six pack abs with the v that makes women weak in the knees. He had thick dark hair over most of his chest, which became sparser as it moved down his torso, culminating in a happy trail that lead to a huge thick cock. His pubic area was well groomed and neatly trimmed. I believe that if you keep the hedges trimmed the trees look taller. Wink, wink.

Paul drew in a sharp breath as Ms. Lovely dropped to her knees on the mattress to take Mr. Lovely's penis in her mouth. I watched as he shifted his own penis through his pants. He apparently wished he were on the receiving end of those luscious lips. I didn't blame him. She was a beauty.

The First Time

I'm not sure if it was the drink, the atmosphere of the place, or the beauty of the couple, but I was very wet. I decided to shed some of my inhibitions for Paul. I maneuvered my chair so it was at an angle facing him, yet I could still see the show. I propped both my feet up on the rung of the table bent my knees slightly and hiked my dress up, exposing myself to him. I saw his pupils dilate and his nostrils flare instantly. A sure sign he was aroused. I began to touch myself for him. I also shifted the slit in the neckline of my dress so my left breast was exposed. I tweaked my nipple with my left hand, and masturbated with my right.

"Yeah Baby," Paul grunted throatily. "Touch that thing for me." I obliged. I let my head lean back, arching my back slightly, for his viewing pleasure.

It was only a couple of minutes before Paul unzipped his pants and let his cock spring free. It was rock hard and ready to go. He began to pump himself with his left hand, slowly at first, but growing increasingly rapid by the moment. We both got caught up in our own pleasure, we were swept away. We had never done this so publically before.

I was running two fingers over and around my clit. It felt so good. I plunged both fingers into my slit and Paul sucked in a ragged breath.

It was hot and moist, and with every pull back of my fingers, some of my juices slid down my taint to my ass puddling on the towel beneath me. I could tell Paul was getting close to the edge. He was throwing his head back and groaning low in his throat. The head of his penis was dark purple with his engorgement.

I don't know what made me do it, maybe it was the sensation of being watched, but I rolled my head to look at Mr. and Ms. Lovely. They were no longer engaged in their own scene but were watching ours. I almost stopped what I had been doing, but something made me continue. Let them look I thought.

To Paul, I whispered, "Babe, they are watching us." He opened his eyes and stopped his motion, but only for a second. He saw that I was still taking care of myself.

"Let them watch then," he whispered back. His voice strained with his impending climax.

My own orgasm hit me like a ton of bricks just then. I plunged both fingers in and out of my pussy at a feverish pace. My other hand left my breast to rub my clit. I tried to keep my noises at a minimum to no avail. As my orgasm took control, I threw my head back and moaned, bucking my hips to match the rhythm of my hands. I arched my back lifting my ass slightly off the chair. Liquid flowed from me dripping onto the towel. I continued to pump my hips as my body was wracked by aftershocks. I heard Paul as he hit his stride. His breathing became labored, then he began to groan. Just in time he used his free hand to pull his shirt up exposing his belly. His cum spurted thickly all over his stomach as he pumped until every last drop had flowed. When he caught his breath, we looked at each other and laughed.

He pulled his shirt over his head and stood up. He came over to me and kissed me gently on the lips. "Do you have any idea how hot you are?" He asked me sincerely.

Being the brat that I was, I said, "Yup, it is pretty friggin' hot in here!"

He laughed. "You know what I mean. Do you have any idea how much I love you right now?"

'Nope. But if you really, really love me, I could use a new drink."

"Done!" He went into the room grabbing the towel from his chair to wipe the jizz off his belly as he went. I used the towel beneath me to wipe myself up a little. I refolded it so the wetness was to the inside and sat back down.

Paul came out of the room in shorts and a T-shirt holding two Beers. He handed me mine. "Thanks, Babe. I need this." As I lifted my drink to my mouth, I noticed the Lovely's standing in the doorway of the play room holding water bottled in the air as if to say cheers to us. We raised our drinks to them and all four of us took a swallow. Ms. Lovely motioned for us to come over. Paul shook his head no, raised his glass again, then took another swig. Undaunted Ms. Lovely just shrugged her shoulders, gave us a pretty little pout, and went back to the mattress. She laid on her back, and beckoned to Mr. Lovely. He hadn't lost an inch of his massive erection. He grabbed Ms. L's ankles, and hoisted her so she was on her upper back with her ass was off the bed. He dropped to his knees, and plunged his face into her bald pussy. He shifted his hands to under her ass, and held her tighter to his face. She began to moan and whine immediately. She threw her head back, and looked at us from her upside down position. Again she crooked a finger in our direction inviting us to join them.

Paul again motioned no. "If we were swingers, I would never say no to that." He mused. "I bet they don't get turned down often."

"I think they are professional swingers," I stated matter-of-factly. "I mean look, they brought their own sheets, towels, and water. They obviously have done this before."

"Professional swingers huh? Do you think there is such a thing?"

"Manuel did tell us to enjoy the show. Maybe

the hotel pays them to keep the party going or something," I suggested.

Ms. L's moans became louder and rhythmic. I could tell she was going to cum soon. Mr. L could too. He pulled his face back, flipped her over, and started pounding her from behind. She moaned and groaned and whimpered as he pumped ever harder into her. Then he pulled out, and positioned his penis at her asshole. He reached between her legs for some of her wetness and slathered it on his dick. With one huge push, he rammed himself into her. As a woman, I know I have to be in practice for that kind of thing. I would never be able to take being slammed like that in the ass. Little by little, and lots of lube, is all that works for this girl. Ms. L. however took it like a champ.

He pounded her ass, over and over. She reached between her legs, and began rubbing her own clit. It was only a matter of seconds before she was in the throes of ecstasy. As her shaking and screams subsided, Mr. L. pulled his member out of her ass, pumped it a few times in his fist, then squirted his cum all over her back. He used his cock to spread the semen around, rubbing it in, then collapsed on the mattress beside her.

After a moment or two, they popped up off the bed, and headed for a door in the back of the room which I had assumed was a closet, duffle bag in hand. They returned through the back door about five minutes later. They were freshly showered and still toweling off. So it wasn't a closet, it was a shower. They pulled comfy sweats for him and yoga pants for her out of the duffle bag, and quickly dressed in them. They both pulled on tank tops. They packed up all their gear, and exited the room, turning off the light as they left. As they stood at the elevator door waiting, Ms. L. turned to us and said, "Too bad. Maybe next time." The elevator doors opened, and they were gone.

Paul and I looked at each other and laughed. We finished our drinks then headed into our room for the night. I threw the towel from my chair on the floor on top of the one Paul had discarded earlier. I pulled my hair up on top of my head and fastened it there. I turned on the shower, got the right temperature, and stepped into the hot water. The new shower curtain pulled to the side as Paul came in with me. He began lathering me up, paying more than necessary attention to my still slick slit. He pushed me up against the shower wall. (Thank goodness it was now clean) I felt his erection at my backside.

"Oh no, Mr. I am not doing that tonight" I warned. He chuckled and shoved me even harder into the tile. He continued to hold me there as he soaped up my back. He reached a hand between my legs and felt I was ready. He found my opening and pushed the head of his cock in with a pop. He held it there for a few seconds using one hand to massage my clit. Then he thrust himself all the way in. I had to raise onto my tip toes, and he had to bend his knees so we fit properly.

He began by pumping in and out slowly. Then his motion became faster and faster. His skillful hand at my clit made me cum on his cock. I almost lost my footing and slipped, but he held me in place with his free arm. The contractions of my vaginal muscles sucked on his dick as it slid in and out. He came inside me, kissing the back of my neck, and telling me he loved me over and over. We finished our shower just as the water started to run cold. We got out, dried off, and plopped into bed, thoroughly exhausted and completely sated. We fell to sleep in each other's arms almost immediately.

We woke to the sound of bottles and cans being dumped from one trash bin into another. It was a loud, obnoxious noise. We could also hear people yelling, though we couldn't exactly make out what they were yelling about. I was on the side of the bed facing the window with Paul comfortably spooned against my back. It seemed too bright in the room. What time was it? I opened one eye and was assaulted by bright sunlight. We had forgotten to draw the blinds. We had also been sleeping on top of the sheets, which I was reminded of, when I saw a pair of elderly naked men standing outside the window leering in at us. I quickly whipped the sheet up over us and roused Paul.

"Babe, Babe! There are men looking in the window!"

"What? What are you saying?"

"There are people looking in the window!"

He sat up. Looked at the pervs touching themselves while looking in the window. He jumped up, and ran to the window, pulled the curtain shut, and screamed "Get the fuck out of here assholes!"

From outside, I could hear them saying "Close the window if you are not putting on a show asshole!"

"Fuck you!" Paul shouted through the now closed window, and stalked into the bathroom slamming the door behind him. The force of the slam knocked the closet door back off of its track, and it fell onto the water heater again.

This place was definitely weird. I hadn't seen the naked perverts the day before. They must be new guests today. I wondered to myself if I should I report them to the front desk?

I got out of bed and immediately put clothes on. I felt dirty and violated. I put on short shorts, and a tank top. I was slipping on some flip flops when Paul came out of the restroom, zipping his shorts, and grumbling under his breath about being awoken by perverts, and a piece of shit hotel. He jerked the closet door and put it back on the track. He turned to me and said, "Do you want to leave yet?" The irritation was still in his voice.

"No, I don't want to leave, but I do think I will report those jerks to the front desk." I walked over and wrapped my arms around his neck. I kissed him. "Let's go get some breakfast and coffee. I need coffee!"

"Yea, let's do that. And what the fuck was all the crashing and banging, and yelling this morning?" He was back to being pissed. He grabbed the keys and his sunglasses. "Let's go."

We walked down to the beach, hand in hand. We strolled along looking at the beautiful water. We found a café that served breakfast and sat down. A beautiful girl, with a Russian accent, asked what we would like. We both ordered coffee and asked for menus. She returned promptly with steaming mugs of coffee, and the menus. A few minutes later she was back with a pot of coffee in hand refilling our cups. Paul ordered the special which was bacon and eggs with toast and hash browns. I ordered a bagel with lox and cream cheese. Our food was delicious. The coffee was mellow and flavorful. Sitting by the ocean watching the joggers and early risers stroll by is one of my favorite things to do on vacation.

"Happy Birthday," Paul said softly. "I am sorry it isn't going so well."

"What do you mean? It is going great. That was some of the best sex ever last night. How could you think that was bad? I almost forgot today is my Birthday."

"That was some mind blowing sex. Thank you, Baby."

"Thank you? Since when do you thank me for sex?"

"I meant thank you for being so cool about all this weirdness, but thanks for the great sex too!" His smile was back.

We finished our breakfast and spent some time on the beach. We walked back to the hotel, stopping at the front desk to complain about the perverts and the morning noise. We were not quite politely informed, that we were the ones in the wrong. That the commonly known rules of 'on premises' swinger places were; if a door is open, you can come in. If a window is open, enjoy the show. Single men are by invitation only, and no means no. Mystery solved. "We are not swingers. How are we supposed to know that?" Paul was not happy with the answer we had gotten.

"Why are you here if you are not swingers?" The nasty desk clerk retorted.

"We are nudists and came for the rooftop sunbathing," I said with a slight attitude myself.

The First Time

"What about all the crashing, banging, and yelling first thing this morning? Are there special swinger rules about that?"

"It is the cleaning crew. They start at 7. If you have a problem with the noise, you can take it up with them."

I guess he told me, I thought. "I'll do that thank you." Was all I said. We went to our room, put on our bathing suits, grabbed a couple towels, and headed back to the beach. It wasn't even 9 a.m. yet. The beach was warm and beautiful. I found many shells I didn't have in my collection. Paul and I romped and swam, then laid in the sun to tan a while. When we had enough sand, we headed back to our room. We decided to take some beers up to the pool, so we grabbed a six-pack and some lime wedges, and headed up. When we stepped off the elevator, we were met by loud music and a crowd of people in and around the pool.

We found seats at the bar and had Manuel serve us back our own beer. There was a grill on the deck filled with burgers and dogs. They were being tended by a naked man with a kiss the cook apron around his waist. I am sure that was a health-code violation, but so were so many other things here. There had to be close to sixty people on the roof. Some were sunbathing, some were swimming, some were drinking, but all were naked or very near to it.

We joined in the nakedness, sitting on our towels at the bar. We chatted with people as they came to the bar. They were from all over. They were all swingers and proud of it. None of them were beautiful like Mr. and Ms. Lovely from last night. In fact, the majority were older, much older than us. Most of the bodies were not tight or toned. Things sagged and bunched in the most inglorious ways. It made Paul and I look like veritable rock stars.

It didn't take long for us to start getting propositioned by, what seemed like, every person there. We begged off kindly, explaining that we were going to have to leave soon to go to the Hard Rock for a comedy show. That was the truth. One, not too bad looking, mid-fiftyish couple asked what our SLS or SDC name was. I was mystified.

"What is that?" Paul asked. The couple explained that they were swinger sites online, where like-minded couples could browse photos and set up 'dates'. There were chat rooms, and event postings. It sounded interesting if you were into that. We weren't. They gave us their card and asked us to stay in touch. They actually had a business card which touted them as Tina and Tony; a fun loving couple, in the lifestyle, looking for new friends and new adventures. I guess there is such a thing as a professional swinger after all.

We took a quick swim, chatted with a few

more people, and then went to our room to dress. We left for the Hard Rock dressed to the nines, Florida style. When we got there, it wasn't quite time for the show, so we grabbed a drink at one of the many bars on the Casino campus. I was feeling mildly buzzed, and euphoric. We paid our bill, tipped the bartender and headed for the comedy show line. The line was very long when we got there, but Paul whisked me past the crowd to the VIP entrance. I was thrilled. We were shown to our seat which was a table nearly dead center in front of the stage. Our waiter took our drink order. When he came back with our beers, he asked which dinner choice we had made. I hadn't seen a menu. Paul took charge and said we would have the prime rib and lobster. The waiter smiled, asking what temperature we liked our prime rib. Rare for me, and medium for Paul. The waiter left, and we talked about our weekend so far as the crowd filed in.

The food was delicious! The beer was cold, and the comedy was tons of fun. We saw Alonzo Morning and Lisa Lampanelli. My funny bone was split by the end of the show. I had a 'per-ma-grin' stuck on my face. On the way back to the Hotel, we stopped at a fancy restaurant for dessert and coffee. Paul chose cheesecake, and I ordered Key Lime pie. We fed each other bites of our dessert. We held hands, and kissed tenderly while we talked in hushed tones. It was a nice way to end an excellent date.

Back at the hotel, we took the stairs to help work off the dessert induced, extra calories. As we stepped out of the stairwell, a sight I never expected to behold was there in front of us. An orgy of at least twenty people, in various sexual positions, was right there in the middle of the second floor. People were sucking, fucking, touching, and teasing. There were girls with girls, guys with guys, threesomes, foursomes, every imaginable sexual combination.

We froze and watched for a minute or two. Then we dashed into our room. We changed into comfy bed clothes. I was in cotton, boy cut undies, and a spaghetti strapped top, and Paul was in pajama bottoms. We grabbed some beer, and quietly took seats at the patio table outside the door. We stayed silent as we watched the orgy. At times I was turned on, at other times I was grossed out. I'd never seen an orgy, except in porn. Real life is not as pretty.

Eventually, members began dropping out of the orgy, one by one. The moans, groans, and grunts subsided, and people drifted away from the central group. Paul and I went to bed exhausted from the long day.

We woke to the familiar crashing of bottles and shouts on Saturday morning. We got dressed

and went back to the same place we had breakfast on Friday. The conversation was all about the
orgy.

"That was really something last night," Paul
said after a sip of coffee.

"Yes, yes it was. I would have bet money I'd
never see anything like that in my lifetime." I mused
and took a sip of my own coffee.

"It was kind of a turn on though, wasn't it?"
he prodded.

"Some of it was. I never thought I would
enjoy watching other people having sex, but I
did. I would have liked it more if any of them
were good looking. I know that sounds vain, but
it is so bizarre seeing so many old, out of shape
people having sex." I couldn't help but be truthful
about my feelings.

"I say more power to them. I hope we are
going at it like that when we are their age."

"I agree. The point is, I just wish it were tighter,
more toned, younger, people we were watching. Some
of the low hanging balls, fat bellies, and floppy tits
just grossed me out. I know we have seen plenty of
naked people, but seeing all their parts in action,
well, some of it just wasn't pretty."

"I totally disagree. I thought all those women
were beautiful in one way or another."

"Really?" I never heard Paul speak like that
before.

"Yeah, I'd do them all." He was serious.

"Wow, married all these years and I never knew that about you."

"Knew what?"

"I never knew you were into older, sloppy women."

"I love all women," he said proudly.

"Oh you do, do you?" I sounded jealous. I knew it.

"You know what I mean. I just think there is something beautiful in every woman, and more so in mothers." He said the last in almost a whisper. I wondered if he was afraid I'd think he was a freak or something. I definitely did not.

"You are so awesome do you know that? I can't believe I am just now seeing this deeper side of you. You never cease to amaze me." I had to stifle a sob as I said that. My eyes were blinking back tears. "I am a horrible person. I thought all those men were pretty disgusting. I wouldn't consider fucking any of them. I guess I am just a stuck up asshole."

"No, you're not stuck up. Those guys were all pretty much trolls." He said it so matter-of-factly that I laughed out loud.

"And what is with the tiny dicks? The words were out before I could filter them.

"I know, right? I certainly have nothing to be ashamed of."

"I never thought you did. Why would you think that?"

Paul has a nice cock, but he is uncircumcised. That made him insecure. When he was growing up, he looked different from the other boys in the locker-room, which incited some teasing. "I don't make a habit out of looking at other men's dicks, but I know a lot of women don't go for the turtleneck."

It had never occurred to me he was this insecure. I had been with Paul since we were teenagers. I just never thought anything was that different. "Really? I never asked around, but why do you suppose women would think that what a flaccid penis looks like is more important than what it looks like hard?"

"I don't know. I just know they do." He sounded almost embarrassed.

"Well, it really doesn't matter what other women think now does it? You are with this woman, and I never even knew you were different until we started getting naked in front of other people. I'd never seen a penis before yours, which I am quite fond of, turtle neck and all." I was.

I had read that uncut men felt quite a bit more sensation during sex. I was happy knowing that was true. Maybe that was why he was always so horny? I liked him that way. I have been considered quite the slut by most of my female friends. Whenever we would enjoy girl talk, they seemed to find fault in their horny husbands, or boyfriends. It was as if they didn't even like sex and could do without it. Not me that is for sure.

The pool party was raging by the time we made it back to the hotel. The grill was filled with various sizzling meats, the music was loud, and the pool itself was full of playing naked bodies. Paul and I joined in the fun. We were chatting with some groups of couples in the pool when I heard someone call.

"Ellie! Hey Ellie, Paul!" Shouting above the noise. It was Tony and Tina, the couple who had given us their business card. They were dressed in their street clothes and were waving to us to come out of the pool and join them. We each grabbed a towel as we climbed out of the pool. We dried off quickly as Tony and Tina made their way over to us through the sun worshipers on the deck. I wrapped myself in my towel sarong style, and Paul wrapped his around his waist.

"Hey guys, we were just leaving, but we wanted to invite you to a party next week in Tampa," Tony said as they neared. "SDC is having a couple's party at a place called the Warehouse. We thought since it is not too far from you, you might make it."

"It is an on premises place with food and a

DJ, but just like here, you bring your own booze and they serve it back to you," Tina added.

"Sounds like fun. Maybe we'll make it." A lie from me. I didn't like to hurt people's feelings.

"Yeah great," Paul smiled. "Maybe we'll see you there."

Tony held out yet another card to Paul. "You have to join SDC to get in. Here is their website info. Once you join, they will send you directions to the club. We gotta get going. We have to pick the kids up by five or her ex holds it over our heads forever. Try and make it. We'll look for you there." Tony was all smiles as he reached out a hand to Paul, who shook it.

Tina had grabbed me in a hug before I realized she was going to. I am a hugger, in general, so I didn't mind. Then she held her arms open to Paul. As he stepped into her embrace, she kissed him on the lips. That I did mind, but I kept it to myself. He looked awkward and embarrassed by it anyway. Tony tried to kiss me as he reached over to hug me, but I turned my cheek so he didn't get my lips.

"It was nice meeting you," we all said almost simultaneously then laughed. With one final wave from Tony, they turned and left the pool area.

Paul put the card with our beach bag, and we got back in the pool. We spent the rest of the afternoon between the pool and sunbathing. We ate the not-so-great barbecue and got very drunk. So drunk, that we ventured into the empty play-room when we returned to the second floor. We closed the door behind us but left the curtains open. We both took turns sitting in the sex swing. I wasn't comfortable in it, so we moved to the black leather mattress.

I was wearing a sheer sarong tied around my neck. Paul wasted no time hiking it out of his way while pushing me backward down onto the bed. He stepped out of his swim trunks quickly. With only our drunkenness, and very minimal, touchy-feely foreplay, we were both already wet and ready. He positioned himself above me on his hands and knees, then slammed himself into me. I was in such a heightened state of arousal, I didn't care that anyone could see us.

"Oh yes, fuck me baby!" I sounded so wanton even to my own ears. I could tell by the look on Paul's face, that he was feeling it too.

"You are so fucking hot! I could cum all over you right now," he growled.

He pulled his cock out of me and crawled to my chest. With his knees straddling me, he held his shaft toward my face. I obliged suck-ing it in deeply. I can control my gag reflex very well. I never liked the forced gagging, or need-ing to spit, like I had seen some of the porn stars do. Paul confided that it was a turn-off to him to see a girl choking and nearly vomiting on a guy's cock, so I never tried to do that. (Don't get me wrong, I can deep throat all of him, and he quite enjoys that.) So I licked and sucked on his engorged manhood, swirling my tongue around the head and licking at his frenulum. I nipped him gently with my teeth making sure not to drag them. I sucked his balls and licked his taint. He was on fire and I knew it. Just as I thought he might cum in my mouth, he pulled himself free from me. He backed himself down my body until he was standing on the floor again. He grabbed my thighs and pulled me toward him until I was barely still on the mattress, my ass half off. He flipped me over to enter me from behind.

There at the window was a young man, mid to late twenties I guessed. I froze, someone was watching. Eep! He was well built. He was shirt-less revealing a hairless chest, and six pack abs with the deep V cuts on the side. He was bald like Paul and heavily tattooed. His board shorts were untied, and he was holding his massive cock in his fist pumping it slowly. He was so close to the glass that if it weren't there, he could have put it in my mouth. I was fixated on his cock. It was thick as well as long. I could actually see a drop of precum escape its head.

Paul snapped me out of my reverie by grabbing my hair, and pulling my head up. I locked eyes with the young man. I could clearly see the desire in them. Paul pushed his cock into me and a jolt of pleasure tore through me. I rolled my head back and moaned, never losing eye contact with my admirer.

"You like it when someone else watches me fuck you?" Paul asked.

"Yes," I whimpered.

Paul pounded me from behind, as the man on the other side of the glass jerked himself off to our rhythm. Tiny rivers were running down my inner thighs. I began to feel the impending onset of an orgasm. The familiar tingles deep in my core getting stronger with each of Paul's thrusts.

"Oh baby, I am gonna cum."

"That's right, cum for me. I want you to cum all over me." He growled into my ear

With Paul's words, I tipped over that mindless edge. Wave after wave of pure pleasure pulsed through my body. I felt it the moment Paul began to cum inside me. The warmth spread into my womb, and gave renewed life to my subsiding ecstasy. At the same time, window guy started pumping thick spurts of semen onto the glass from the outside. We were all lost in our own noises of pleasure.

Thoroughly sated, I collapsed onto my belly on the bed. Paul let go of my hair and he too collapsed onto the mattress, on his back beside me. Window guy stuffed his slowly deflating member back into his shorts, and with a mock tip of the hat, he left. As our breathing returned to normal, we both began to laugh.

"Well, that was different," Paul said through a giggle.

"Yes, it was. Are you mad at me?"

"Mad, for what?"

"I don't know, getting turned on by some strange guy whacking off, practically in my face?"

"It did turn you on didn't it? It turned me on watching you get turned on by it." He always knew what to say to make me feel better. No wonder I love him so much!

"I think it's this place. There is just so much sex going on here, it is hard not to get caught up in it."

"You might be right, or maybe it's just you. Maybe you are a little kinky freak." He joked.

"You might be right." I threw his own words jokingly back at him as I got up and adjusted my sarong, which had become just a mass of material around my neck. "Either way, that is one for the record books I think. How often do you suppose three people all cum at the same exact moment?"

"I don't know, it was pretty cool though." Paul pulled on his bathing suit, and grabbed our beach bag. We crossed the courtyard to our room.

I straightened up and repacked our bags

as Paul took a shower. When he was done, it was my turn. I let the heat of the water soak deep into my bones as I re-ran our encounter in my mind. What would it be like to be with another man? I had only ever been with Paul. Only ever really wanted Paul. What would the aftermath of such an encounter be? Would Paul still love me even if it were a consensual thing? Would I still love myself? I let it all drift away as my muscles became loose, and the dried proof of sex washed away with the soap and water.

We sat on our bed with the window blinds open. We turned the TV on for good measure, although we weren't actually watching it. Paul had opened two beers for us, and we talked and drank while relaxing.

Paul asked, "So would you ever consider being a swinger? I am not saying I would or wouldn't, I just want to know what you think."

"No. Yes. I don't know. I never would have even thought about it before this weekend. I have never been into the idea of being unfaithful."

He posed, "Would it still be unfaithful if we were both okay with it?"

"I guess not. It really is a turn-on having other people watch. I wonder what it would be like to have other people join in." So there it was, I was open to it.

"We could give it a try, and if it isn't for us,

just go back to being not swingers."

"Isn't that like trying to put the genie back in the bottle though? I mean you can't undo it if one of us ends up getting hurt." Wise words I thought, even if I do say so myself.

"We'd have to make a pact that no-one would get hurt and we'd have to stick to it. No jealousy. No name calling, no fighting, no silent treatment, no leaving. If we do this, we do it as a team. If only one of us likes it and the other doesn't, the one who wants out wins."

The idea seemed logical. "I guess that could work. I don't know. I never met swingers before, as far as I know, so I don't know how all this works, or doesn't. It's not like we have anyone we can ask."

"Well, if you want to test it out, I think we have a place to start."

"What? What do you mean a place to start?" My nerves jumped to life immediately.

"That guy, from before, the one who was watching, I'm pretty sure he wants you."

"Oh really, why do you say that?"

"He has passed by our window at least five times since we have been sitting here."

"Really? I saw him go by before, but I don't think he wants to hook up with us."

"See for yourself." He pulled me up off the bed and out the room door. He motioned with his head slightly for me to look up to the side.

There he was, window guy. He was on the third floor almost directly across from our room. He had a T-shirt on now, but was still wearing the same board shorts as earlier. He was leaning over the rail with a beer in one hand, just hanging out. When he saw me look up at him, he raised his beer can in a mock toast to us. Paul and I both held our beers up to him. Then I turned on my heels, and practically ran back into our room. Paul followed closely behind.

"What's the matter with you? I thought we were going to try this."

"I don't know. I'm nervous. I don't think I can do this." Window guy walked by our room again.

"See, he wants you. The ball is in your court Baby."

"Balls, you mean balls. I don't have any right now." My nerves were on hyper drive. "Okay, okay what do I do?"

"I don't know, I am not going to pimp for you. You have to reel him in yourself. Go talk to him, or wave to him or something."

"I can't. What would I say? Oh my god this is crazy." I stepped over to look out the window. I could see him on the fourth floor walking. I sat back on the bed. He was still out there, but he is up on another floor. "Open the door."

The First Time

"What? Open the door, why?" Sometimes Paul could be dense.

"The rules remember. Closed means watch, open means join." He opened the door slightly and sat on the bed with me.

We both pretended to watch TV, but we were waiting. Waiting for some stranger to take the hint and come into our room. I couldn't help but feel self-conscious. Did I look and smell appealing? What would he want to do? Would we kiss, fuck, or just touch and pet and stuff? My head was spinning. How does one orchestrate a ménage a trois? I guessed we would find out.

I saw him before Paul did. He was on the other side of the courtyard looking in the play-room. Was he watching another couple now? I could see both his hands were at his sides, so he wasn't pleasuring himself this time. He turned around. Did he feel me watching him? He started walking toward our room. I held my breath. He walked right by. He briefly glanced in and smiled, but he walked right by. Well, that was that. He would have come in if he were interested right? So I got up closed the door, shut the blinds, and we went to bed.

I woke up to a beautiful day, a tiny twinge of disappointment, and mostly relief. My virtue, so to speak, was still intact. We were leaving soon, so I went up for one last look at the view from the roof, as Paul loaded the car. I was leaning on the railing enjoying the breeze when a voice in my ear whispered "Too bad." I spun and came face to face with window guy. He really was gorgeous.

"I waited for you," he said.

"I uh, um, we opened our door," was all I could squeak out.

"Did you? I didn't see it open." He smiled. "Maybe later?"

"We're leaving in a few minutes, sorry."

"So I was right, too bad. Maybe another time." With that he walked away.

I watched him as he went to the other side of the pool and sat down on a chaise lounge. A beautiful, young, petite, blonde, who was sunbathing naked on the chair next to his, sat up and they kissed. His girl? His wife? Paul would have liked to have that wrapped around his cock, I thought. I went back downstairs and we left.

Somewhere on Alligator Alley we had 'the talk'. We have come to learn that every swinger couple has the talk. We laid out the rules. Our rules for how we would be able to be swingers and preserve our relationship.

Rule 1-No deep kissing. For me, it was too personal, and too open to infection. Rule 2-Same room only. We had to be within arm's reach, and eye contact with each other at all times. Rule 3-No friends. We didn't need to have relationships with people we just wanted to use for sex. Rule 4-VETO power. We could each call a veto if we didn't want the other with someone that bothered us, for any reason, at any time, and the other had to comply. Rule 5-No Family involvement. We would never tell anyone in our family and would never expose them to it at all. Rule 6-Safe sex only. Condoms were a must at all times. No involvement with drug users, or anyone with known transmittable disease even with condoms. Rule 7-No falling in love! We would not spend more than brief, fleeting encounters with virtual strangers, so no emotional bonds could be made. Rule 8-Even if it were true; no-one could be said to be better at anything sexual, than either of us was. To each other, or to others we talked to, no one was better, as far as we were concerned. Rule 9-No fighting or drama. With each other or anyone we chose to share with, and no regrets. Most important, rule 10-If, at any time, either of us wanted to stop swinging, that was it, the end. This was supposed to enhance our relationship not change us.

We made it home and went about the business of being us for a couple days. Then one evening Paul called me into the home office. He was sitting at the computer typing as I walked in.

"Look at this. This is that website Tony and Tina gave us with that Warehouse party invite. You are not going to believe how many people are into this Babe."

A Birthday Surprise

I looked over his shoulder and saw what looked like a list of photos of mostly naked, or nearly naked woman and couples, and genitalia. I was intrigued. We spent hours looking at profiles of swingers, advertising their likes and availability. They had photographs, mostly of the women, vital statistics, like height, weight, age, and even hair style. They had preferences for women, men, couples, or more. They specified things like smokers or non-smokers, tattoos, piercings, and height weight proportionate. It was fascinating. There were so many, thousands, maybe more.

"How did you get on here?" I asked.

"I signed us up and made a profile," he replied proudly.

"What?! I don't want people to see us on here. My job, your job, our family!" I was mortified.

"Calm down. I made us a private name and I didn't put any pictures on it. I just wanted to get the invite to that party. You have to be members to get directions." He was mildly irritated with me. "Here look, I put us on the list for the party. They sent directions to our in-box." We checked out the directions and shut down the computer.

Back in the living room we talked about going to a swinger party. We decided we at least wanted to check it out. "We'll get a hotel nearby so we don't drink and drive, and we'll just see how it goes."

The First Time

The days flew by till it was time to go to the Warehouse. We drove up to Tampa, checked into the hotel which was walking distance from the club. It actually looked just like a warehouse in a warehouse district. A small sign designated it as a club. We went out to dinner. We stopped at a liquor store on the way back to the hotel. We bought a bottle of Patron Silver, a twelve pack of Corona Light, and some limes, then went back to the room to dress for the night.

I wore a halter dress which barely covered my ass. It clung to all my curves and looked too hot for daywear. It made my legs look longer than they are. A pair of bright red, pleather, stripper pumps, with five inch clear heels, completed the outfit. Paul wore black slacks and a black, short sleeved, button up shirt. He looked yummy! We drove the short distance to the Warehouse so we wouldn't have to carry the booze.

Bright neon signs flashing sex, sex, sex were illuminating the club in Technicolor. As we walked in the door, we were greeted in what appeared to be a small anti-room, by a barrel-chested man in a suit. The room was all black. The walls were draped in black velvet. There was a small counter in front of us which was illuminated by twinkling lights. There was a fish bowl filled with multi-colored condoms, next to a cash register, and a clipboard. Money changed hands, papers were signed, and he looked our names up on the invitation list (clipboard). He took our drinks, tagged them with our name. They were sent away, in the arms of a young, thin, black man, who appeared as if on cue, to some unknown place behind the door. He then proceeded to put neon yellow, wristbands on us, as he ran down the rules.

"Yellow is for couples, pink is for singles, he announced. No sex on the dance floor or at the bar, anywhere else is fine. If a door is closed, don't go in. If a door is open, whatever. Towels are in the locker room, so are showers. There are bathrooms on either side of the bar. Waitresses work for tips only, be kind. Oh, no means no. Any questions?"

"No, that about covers it," Paul said as the man pulled back a thick curtain to admit us.

We walked down a long, dark corridor. There was a door at the end with a sign on the door which read: No one under twenty-one allowed. If nudity or sexual activity is in any way offensive to you, do not pass through this door. We opened the door to what looked like a regular club. There was techno music playing. Multiple flat screen TV's showed nude shadow dancers swaying in time to the music. The bar extended in an L shape around two back walls. There were disco balls throwing colored orbs all around. A stripper pole was the center of the large dance floor. A DJ booth sat high on the side of the dance floor perpendicular to the bar. Beautiful nudes were the designer's choice of wall décor.

We found seats at the bar. A perky young waitress introduced herself as Carly and opened our beer for us. We surveyed the bar as we drank. There was a door under the DJ booth. We watched as couples drifted through the doors. Some returned, some didn't. As we chatted and drank, we kept an eye out for Tina and Tony.

Paul left to go to the restroom. A man came over and sat on my opposite side. Carly got him his drink, and they engaged in idle chit-chat. I was turned in my seat facing the dancefloor. The man next to me leaned close to my ear and said "Red is a good color for you. My name is Paul how are you?"

"Thank you, Paul, I am fine. My name is Ellie. My husband's name is also Paul that's him coming over here.

Paul walked gracefully back to me across the dance floor carefully dodging dancers as he did. He had a grin on his face which made me laugh. He raised a quizzical eyebrow as he watched the other Paul lean back toward me.

"You have a very sexy laugh Ellie." I laughed again.

"Paul, this is Paul I said, introducing my husband to the man sitting next to me. They shook hands and Paul took his seat. I turned back to face the bar. Paul asked Carly to set us all up with a shot of patron. We each took a slice of lime Carly handed us, then licked our wrists and salted them up. With our drink hand, we all said "Cheers", and clinked glasses. We threw down the burning liquid, licked the salt off our wrists, and then bit the lime. We settled into a pleasant conversation.

Three shots in, I had to find the restroom. I followed the neon sign which lead through the door under the DJ booth. It was another long corridor, but this one had many doors on either side. I could hear the sounds of sex emanating from behind the doors. Some of the doors had windows. I could see various groups engaged in multiple sex acts through the windows. Some of the rooms had themes like jungle, dungeon, and outer space. Most were just dimly lit rooms with mattresses on the floor. I found the door to the restroom. There was a line of course.

On my way back from the restroom, an older balding man asked if I would like to join him in the dungeon room. "Not tonight darling," I said as I sashayed by, swinging my hips for extra measure. I made my way back to the bar and Paul. Both Paul's were leering at me as I walked up. "What?"

"Paul wants to know if we would like to invite him back to one of the rooms with him," Paul said.

The First Time

"I can't see why not," I said rather flippantly. I was mildly annoyed that they had been talking about such things without me. I wasn't sure I really wanted to, but this is what we came here for, and all the overt sex and booze had me pretty wet. So we all three headed to the corridor if rooms.

"This one looks as good as any," I pulled the door open to the first empty room I came to. Inside there was a mattress on the floor, and a pile of clean sheets in the corner. There was a small table with various sample size lubes and a bowl of condoms. It was all we needed.

I pulled off my shoes and whipped the red dress off over my head. I hadn't worn any underwear, a 'no lines' look to my form fitting dress. The men began to undress.

My Paul was a sexy man. He had a beautiful body for his age. He always had a slim, muscular build. The other Paul was the same age as us. He was a little, yet not disturbingly so, overweight. When his clothes came off I was pleased to see, he didn't have a tiny dick. It wasn't huge, it was average I guess, but nice and thick.

I got on my knees in front of him and began to suck his cock. The size and even texture felt different from my Paul. His taste was different too. I licked and sucked like a girl with her favorite lollipop. Not to be left out for too long, my Paul pulled me into a doggie position, while I kept my attention on the cock in my mouth. Paul placed himself on his knees behind me, and slowly slid his hard member into my tight hot slit. I began to rock with the rhythm of both men. One fucking me from behind, one fucking my face.

"She sucks cock like a pro," Paul to my Paul.

"Yes, she does! She fucks like a porn star with this tight little pussy of hers," Paul smacked my ass playfully as he said that. "Wanna switch?"

My Paul pulled himself out of me. I spun around and took his juice slicked cock in my mouth as the other Paul took me from behind.

"Oh man you're right, she does have a tight little pussy." He started to massage my ass and reach around to my clit. He dipped his fingers into the wetness he found between my legs, then slid his thumb into my ass.

I felt myself getting close to the edge. Ripples of pleasure were coursing through my body. The tingles were starting to ignite in my core. Paul could tell by my noises, and inability to stay focused on sucking him that I was getting close. He pulled away from me. He sat on the low mattress, and beckoned me to him, so I obliged. Moving myself gently away from the sweet torture of the other Paul, and my impending orgasm, I climbed onto the mattress and up over my husband, I lowered my sex onto his hard shaft. The other Paul came up behind me and rubbed his dick in my ass crack. Having already been teased to a near frenzy by his thumb, I said, "Oh yes, fuck my ass too. I want both of you in me at once."

"Let me grab some lube. Be right back." He found one of the sample tubes on the small table.

I could smell the scent of the lube as soon as he tore the package open. He poured a generous amount into his hands and greased his cock up. Then he moved closer and poured some of the tingling liquid down the crack of my ass. It ran down between my legs and into my pussy. My Paul felt it too, as the slightly warming sensation hit his shaft from inside me.

"Oh yea, that feels so good, you like that Baby? God, that feels so good."

"I like it, it is so hot and tingly. My pussy is on fire."

The other Paul took a fistful of my hair and moved over my back. He positioned his penis at my asshole. Slowly, at first, he slid in with the help of the lube. Pain mixed with pleasure, as the tingling inside me came from a deeper, different place than before.

"Oh god, yes that's it! I want you both inside me. Fuck my ass! Fuck my pussy! That's it! I feel so full. I am going to cum!"

I am not sure if it was my vocal commands or just the nature of the beast, both Paul's started driving into me faster and faster. Fireworks and sparkles were shooting off all over my body. I could feel my eyes rolling back in my head. I am sure my noises became more primal as coherent thought became a thing of the past.

"This is so fucking hot! Your ass is so hot and tight, I am going to cum! Oh shit, I am so close!" It was obvious the other Paul was nearing orgasm as well.

"I'm right there with you. This is fucking awesome!" My Paul said. He looked into my eyes, then kissed me passionately.

My body let loose. Contractions in my ass and pussy sent millions of pleasure sensations rippling through my body from the core out. "I'm cumming, I'm cumming!" I screamed. "Oh shit, aahhhhh!" Over the edge I fell. I could hear both Paul's grunting and groaning, as I whimpered in pleasure.

"Fuck! I'm cumming! Shit! Fuck! Aaaggghhh!" Although I couldn't feel him cum in my ass due to the condom, I knew Paul was climaxing too. He withdrew. My body felt the loss. My Paul kept pounding into me and aftershocks of pleasure continued to wrack my body.

A few more hard pumps and Paul was there. "Oh fuck yeah Baby! You are so hot and amazing, I'm cumming! Oh, grrr, I'm cumming!" He growled out. He forced his hips up into me one last time and went still. "Aagghhh!" He collapsed back into the mattress taking me with him. The other Paul sat down beside us.

Our breathing all returned to normal, and we all began to chuckle.

"Well, that was fucking amazing. Thank you, both. I'm not sure what to do here." He motioned to the full condom hanging off his quickly fading erection. We all laughed some more. "I guess I have to find the restroom."

He got up and wrapped a sheet around his waist. He extended a hand to Paul, who sat up and returned his shake. "Thanks again man." I sat up as well. To me, he said, "Ellie, you are so hot. I hope we can do this again sometime." He leaned down to kiss me and I turned to offer a cheek. I just smiled. He gathered his clothing and left the room.

Paul leaned over and planted a big wet kiss on my lips. "Was that good for you?"

"What do you think? Of course, it was good. I had multiple orgasms didn't I?"

"Just making sure you're okay Babe, that's all."

"I'm fine, but I need a drink and I have to clean up." I pulled my dress over my head, slipped my shoes back on, and waited by the door as Paul finished dressing.

He grabbed the sheets off the bed, wadded them into a ball, and took them with us as we exited the room. We went into the locker room, dropped the sheets in a laundry basket, put our clothes on a bench, and then stepped into a hot shower. We soaped each other up and rinsed off keeping it pretty PG. We were both exhausted. I was losing my buzz. We decided against the drink and left, forgetting to take our booze with us. We drove back to the hotel even though we shouldn't be driving.

I collapsed onto the bed feeling queasy and insecure. The more the alcohol wore off, the worse I felt, both physically and emotionally. Paul had passed out and begun to snore almost immediately. I lie awake for a while. I felt dirty, like I did something wrong, yet when I replayed the threesome in my mind, I still got turned on. I fell into a fitful sleep.

When I awoke in the morning, my head was pounding! I felt instantly sick and had to run to the bathroom to throw up. I retched and retched until there was nothing left in my stomach. Paul was sitting on the bed when I came out of the bathroom.

"No Bueno huh?" He asked.

"No. No, Bueno." I sat next to him, grabbed one of the pillows and started to cry into it.

"Oh Baby, what's the matter?" Paul asked pulling the hair back from the side of my face and tucking it behind my ear.

I couldn't answer. I just sobbed, and sobbed,

as Paul petted my hair and back, and waited out whatever I was going through. When I could finally speak, I looked at him. With the tears still flowing, I tried to explain.

"I feel bad about what we did last night. I've never been with anyone but you, and that was precious to me. What if it is a sin? What if it is wrong? I can never have that back." I began to sob again. I felt heartbroken. Would Paul ever feel the same about me as he had before? How had I let such a bizarre kink into our marriage, our lives?

"Look at me Baby." Paul cupped my face in his hands. With his thumbs, he tried to wipe the tears that flowed freely. "I love you. That hasn't changed. I will never think less of you for what we did." He emphasized the 'we.' "I was there too remember?"

I tried to say something, but all that came out was a hiccup and a squeak. We both chuckled.

"You gave me your virginity. I get to keep that gift forever. It doesn't go away because of what we did. Besides, I don't want to believe in a god who thinks sex and having fun, between consenting adults, is a sin."

"I know, but…" My voice hitched as the sobs tried to take over.

"No, buts. Did you have a good time?"

"Yes. It was a fantasy that came to life."

"For me too. I had a great time. Remember the rules, no regrets right?" I shook my head in acknowledgment. "If you don't want to do it again we won't. But I do have to say, that was the hottest sex we have had in a long time, and that is actually saying something."

"Yea, it was hot, wasn't it?" I was feeling better. He calmed my fears and made me whole and right again. I smiled as I looked into his eyes and saw only love.

We reached for each other at precisely the same moment. We hugged so tightly, for so long. After what could have been minutes or hours, our hug turned into a kiss. The kiss deepened as true love and passion flowed between us. We made love, beautiful, passionate, romantic, love. No regrets, no second-guessing, no one else. It was perfect and it was the best sex of my life.

SAMANTHA'S WRITING IS SO REAL YOU WON'T BELIEVE ITS FICTION

Black Widow Books

Me
& My Nympho

VISITING A
SWINGER CLUB
TO PICK UP
ANOTHER GUY

MEETING A STRANGER TO GET DP

WRITNER

Me and My Nympho

Samantha Writner

My new girlfriend is quite crazy in the bed-room. A true nympho in just about every sense of the word. What guy doesn't want that? She doesn't always let me fuck her ass. Sometimes, if I can get her amped up just right though, she actually begs me for it.

We were both rather new to the town we lived in. I guess that was one thing that connected us in the beginning. Then, there was the sex. Unbelievably great!

I was surprised to find out that she really hadn't had too many experiences with more than one person at a time. She had been with another woman when she was pretty young, and her first threesome was with a man and a woman, immediately followed by another with two men. Since then though, she said she hadn't really done anything else.

I have had my share of threesomes in the past, as well as straight up orgies. I actually used to have a membership to a swingers club. That was great. All the dark rooms filled with writhing bodies, and the smell of sweat and sex. It was a candy shop for a guy like me. I could find a room and watch a bit. Then if the inhabitants wanted me, they'd invited me in. I developed a reputation, and was almost always invited into any room I wanted.

I got the idea that maybe we could see if this new town had any swinging places. Having a threesome with Stephanie would be great. It's a small town, so I wasn't sure about anything being here. Not that Stephanie wasn't enough, because she could fuck for hours, non-stop! I figured, I had better ask Steph if she was interested first.

We were in the throes of our nightly horizontal workout when I decided to ask. "So, do you want to have another person join us some time?"

She had just finished polishing my knob, and was about to use the glistening saliva to ease it into her pussy. "What? Sure. Why? You can't handle me anymore? You need help?" She laughed as she began a slow rockin' on my cock.

"No. I've still got my energizers running. I just thought we would add to the party. You've done it before, I've done it before, why not go again? It would be a first for us together."

"Ok." Her breathing increased as her mastery of bringing herself to orgasm was precision. "Well, shut up and fuck me harder now! There's no one else here at the moment, and I'm about....to.... cum. Ah yes! Right there!"

I responded to her request by grabbing her hips, and forcefully sliding her across my pelvis, providing clitoral stimulation while I raised my hips to thrust my cock inside her. She loved the end to be quick and hard, and I knew exactly how to give it to her. "Yes baby. Cum for me. Slide that wet pussy and cum on my cock."

He body began to go limp as the orgasm sapped her strength. I stopped moving her on me, and felt her body quiver with spasms.

She lay down on me, breathing heavy. "God your cock is amazing."

"Your pussy is pretty damn fine too." I moved her off me, and moved to take her from behind.

She spread her legs obediently, knowing how I loved it. I slid my cock into her and began pounding feverishly. Her hips arched against me, and the pressure of her walls tilted against my head brought me quickly to finality.

I jumped up from the bed and went to the bathroom, returning with a warm wash cloth to gently clean my jizz off her.

She smiled at me. "So you want more people, huh?"

I shrugged, "I don't care. I just know how insatiable you are. I thought it would be a good change. You know, so we don't ever go stale."

"Sure. Where you gonna find them? You're right, I'm up for anything."

"Ok. I wanted to make sure you were ok with it before I go hunting to see if this place has anything like that."

"Like what?"

"A lifestyle club. It's where swingers hang out."

She was a bit surprised by that answer, and giggled a bit. "Wow. I didn't know they actually had clubs for nymphos."

"Yep. I'm kind of surprised you aren't a veteran member." I chucked the wash cloth at the clothes hamper, jumped back onto the bed, and gave her a quick peck.

"Yeah, right! Well, let me know." She continued with a slight pause, "You staying here tonight?"

"I'd love to."

We snuggled into the sheets together and drifted off to sleep. No strings attached we said.

It only took me one search on the internet to find it. SDC.com lists all active clubs around the world. There was a meet and greet hosted by SDC this coming weekend at a club called TBL, Total Bottom Line.

I looked up the club and found out it was normally a gay club, although they seemed to have lots of different types of parties. Gay clubs always have the best dance music too, I thought to myself. I figured it was as good a place to meet people as anywhere else.

After I got off work I ran back to my place to grab some stuff. I rented a room from this woman who had the 'hots' for me and I didn't want to be there when she got home. Way too many strings attached there.

I grabbed about half my shit, and then headed to the bar where Steph and I had met a few months back. We regularly met up there ever since. As soon as she got off work, and changed out of her work clothes, she would head there too. I was kind of excited to tell her what I had found. We could be slammin' some home runs by this weekend.

I was half way through my second beer when she walked in. Damn, she is so hot. There is something I can't put a finger on about a woman who loves to fuck. Maybe they walk different, hold their head a little different, and lick their lips more often than other women… I don't know, but she definitely had it.

I raised my hand, "Hey Steph. Over here."

She heard my voice as her eyes adjusted from the blazing sun outside, to the darkness of our favorite tavern. Trusting her senses, she headed my direction.

Tammy had a second beer on the bar already as Steph took her seat, and I went in for a quick kiss. Steph didn't always like public displays, as we were technically not an item.

"Thanks Tammy," she said. To me, "How was your day?"

"Work was good. Hard work makes a hard body." I flexed my bicep for her to punctuate my statement. She was a retired professional athlete. I knew how much muscles turned her on, another reason we connected well. "I had some time after, to check out some…uh…other bars we could go to."

She cocked an eyebrow at me, "Oh really now. You are on the ball." She elbowed me playfully. "Ok, tell me what you found. Or, should we wait till we are in private?"

"We're good. There's a…ah…party this weekend. A place to meet people. I thought we would go."

"Ok. What do I wear?"

"Something sexy of course. Not that you couldn't wear a gunny sack and look sexy. It's like advertising. We should work out beforehand too. They love that."

"Oh, so you're the big expert now, huh?" She laughed. I gave myself a point for causing such a beautiful sound. "Ok. We'll go and check it out. Let's play some billiards. You ready to lose today?"

We played for a few hours, before retiring to our evening sexual escapades.

She was ripping my clothes off before we made it in the front door. "You want to watch another man fuck me?"

"Yes. I want to fuck your ass while he is fucking your pussy."

"Oh! That sounds hot. I want to try that."

"I thought you might be interested in something along those lines. I took the liberty of grabbing some of my porn when I was home today. I have one that you might find particularly exciting." I kissed her, and had to pull hard to get her to let me escape and go to the living room to put the porn into the DVD player.

She was pouty, although I'm pretty sure it was for show. "I don't need any porn to get me excited. I want you to fuck me now."

"We will, we will. I'm gonna fuck you right here on the couch while you watch a DP movie, two guys fucking a girl at the same time. You know, DP, double penetration."

She smiled and continued to remove her clothes

seductively. My attention was split as I tried to fast forward the DVD to the appropriate place. She knelt down in front of me, unfastening my pants. My erection was pushing against the fabric. It sprung to attention as she focused her attentions there.

I found the right place in the movie. "Here. Come sit here and watch this with me." I patted the couch next to me.

She somewhat reluctantly got up and sat next to me. She grabbed my cock as she sat, and slowly kneaded it, while she watched.

On screen was a hot, young blonde in a bra and tiny panties. There were two guys there who had simultaneously dropped their pants in front of her. She over acted her surprise, and immediately went to sucking one and stroking the other.

"Ummmm. That's right." Steph acknowledged her approval by stroking my cock a bit more forcefully. I had to quickly exhale with the pleasure it caused me.

The girl on screen took off her bra as the second guy removed her panties, and stuck his cock inside her. The camera was ping-ponging between her deep throating, and his deep thrusting.

I reached over to massage Steph's clit. She sat back to enjoy, and continued a masterful hand job on me.

The first guy sat down on the couch, and the blonde straddled his cock. The second guy stood on the couch, and instructed the blonde to 'suck it'.

Steph looked over at me and my throbbing piece. Pre-cum had made the head glisten. "I want to suck it."

"Not yet. Keep watching." It was very different for us to hold back, and not jump on each other immediately.

The blonde stood and turned around, then slammed her asshole onto the waiting erection. The second guy was now standing in front of her. He lifted her legs, exposing her wet pussy, then thrust his cock in her pussy. The camera angle changed and you could see both cocks fucking in a slick rhythm of lubed sex.

I looked at Steph to see her reaction.

"Oh. Damn. That made me wet." She was now helping me massage her clit. "Oh yeah, fuck it."

Her eyes smiled along with her luscious lips, and I knew she was into it. Her hips flexed with an energized excitment.

She suddenly jumped up and straddled me. Once she had established complete penetration, she turned so she could still see the screen. I wanted to see the blonde stretched to the limit, and so did she. Taking two cocks at the same time. The camera zoomed in and you could see her pussy was running with juices.

The scene changed, they are always so quick.

The First Time

Once Steph realized it wasn't going to show the blonde anymore, she turned her full attention back to fucking me. The corney porn music continued behind her.

"You're right. I want that. I want you to fuck me, and have another cock inside me. Fuck both my holes." She slammed on me over, and over, finally cumming with an onslaught of her own juices running all over me, tickling my balls on the way down. It was so hot, my cock exploded with her, adding to the mess.

I told her I would be by around 6. We could eat, get ready, and then be slightly late to the meet and greet at 9. When I arrived she was in a tizzy though.

"What am I supposed to wear? I have no idea what to expect there. What are you wearing?"

"Calm down. These aren't black tie event people. Not when they are attending these kind of events at least. I have these designer jeans." I pulled my bag off my shoulder and started pulling out my clothes before I could even get the door shut. "...and this blue button down. No biggie, clubbin' clothes."

She looked only slightly relieved. "Oh. Ok

then. I'm going to go take a shower and primp. There is some chicken marinating, ready to be cooked, rice is already finished, and salad is in the fridge." She gave me the quickest hello peck, and was gone.

We don't go out of the house much together. We always seem to be fucking. I guessed this was something she was not used to.

I continued pulling my clothes out of my bag, draped them on the back of a chair, so they wouldn't get any more wrinkled, then proceeded to the kitchen, as directed. I hadn't realized I would be cooking the entire meal myself. Women do take a lot longer to get ready than men, so I complied.

I looked over everything and decided we had a lot of time to kill. I went into the bathroom to see if I could distract her from the later event.

She was already in the shower. She had her foot propped up on the wall, shaving her lower leg. She is amazingly flexible, another quality that I love to brag about.

"So, do you need anyone to help you…ah… primp?"

"I don't know. How good are you at shaving a woman's private parts?"

"Uhhhh…I would have to say amateur. I have never done that part before. I have done legs before though." I was hoping she was mostly finished with her legs so I wouldn't have to spend too much time primping.

"Ok. Then I will let you do the other leg and you can watch while I do my cooch. I wouldn't want any mishaps down there with the slip of a razor."

I cringed. "Ouch! No."

I quickly jumped out of my clothes and hopped in the shower with her. "So, how should we do this? I've always been in a bath when I did it before."

"You can sit in the tub. Pretend you are in a bath."

Chuckling, I sat. "Bird's eye view from here." I reached out and ran a finger through the slit between her legs.

She handed me the razor and soap, and waggled a finger at me. "Now, now... Not yet. We have to save that for later."

I stopped moving. "What? We don't have to wait until later. We have hours before we even have to leave. Then it will take at least two hours before we solidify anything with anyone. Come on. I know you are horny. You're always horny."

She smiled at me and motioned for me to begin my task.

"I'm serious. This is just a meet and greet. There is a possibility we won't fuck anyone else tonight. It's not like the club I was in up north.

They had rooms and everything at the club, it's called an 'on-premises' club. This one down here is just hosting an event, no fucky on the premises."

"You've been to this one before?"

"No. I looked up all the info about it the day I went searching. It's a gay club."

"Well, at least they will have good music."

"Yeah, I thought the same thing." My mind was zeroing in on my task. I didn't want to cut her. "If I do a good job here, can I at least get a quickie before dinner?"

She laughed. "A 'quickie'?" She emphasized the word with quoting fingers in the air. "For you that means what...? Only half an hour?" She grabbed the razor from me. "Better let me do the rest or we won't have time for your quickie."

I sat back and watched her quickly finish her leg and then move to her pussy. She spread her lips in a few different ways, first lifting her leg, then with her hands, then bending over. It was like some erotic, mating ritual dance, and it was working on me of course.

She glanced down with a smile as my cock started to spasm to life. I flexed and made it jump for her pleasure. I imagined her warm wetness sliding over it, and it jumped again, voluntarily.

I grabbed the soap that she let drop on the floor, lathered some into my hand, and began stroking my dick.

The First Time

She finished washing as I admired the toned muscles of her legs, butt, and abs. What a specimen she was. And damn, I get to fuck her just about whenever I want.

She turned around to face me, pausing for a brief moment, and then squatted onto my bubbly cock. The soap eased her on, and her powerful thighs flexed to provide a perfect springing action.

Slamming over, and over, her breasts gleefully jumping to the beat. I reached up and grabbed them. Her breathing had increased.

Suddenly she stopped and stood up. "We have to get out of the shower. This tub is too small for any real fun."

She rinsed and grabbed a towel on her way back to the bedroom. I sat for a second, catching my own breath. I had quite a lot more soap suds to rinse off now. I did that as quickly as I could, and I was off to catch her.

I sprung onto the bed between her legs, envisioning myself as a pirate just landing ashore. My sword at the ready.

She laughed and pulled at my hips to come closer. I obeyed.

I started by massaging her clit with the head of my dick, in small, slow circles. Then rubbing it forward and back, still just on the head. Finally, dipping into her slightly, I spread her juices around to ensure everything was wet and ready.

She loved to be teased that way, although we were actually on a time line tonight, so I slammed it as deeply as I could go with no warning.

She cried out with pleasure. "Yes," she whispered as I pulled out.

I slammed it again. Her eyes closed and she writhed with pleasure. Pulling out ever so slowly, then slamming in again with full force. The pleasure it was bringing me was another notch above any we had previously experienced. I knew she was enjoying it too. Our legs were lathered with a new lubricant. Each time I pulled out, more was added, we were soaked.

It was like the crashing waves on the rocks of a cliff, with the gentle pull of the tidal reverse. After a few minutes I couldn't take it anymore. Every time was like a giant firework exploding and all I wanted was more, I wanted it to be constant.

I lifted her hips up slightly to get a grip under her butt and began pumping with maddening speed.

Her breath caught. "Oh! Oh! Yes! Fuck me!"

"Yes, I'm…gonna…fuck…you!" Each word emphasized with the slap of skin.

"Oh yes! You're gonna make me cum."

"Yes. Cum for me." I could feel her pussy walls closing in around me. Squeezing my dick. Sucking on it. She needed to hurry. I wasn't going to be able to hold out much longer. "Oh my god it feels good."

Her body was quivering with ecstasy, and I knew it was time. The grand finale of fireworks went off in my body. Endorphins shot throughout my body, partially paralyzing me, ecstasy... I collapsed on her.

We were definitely a hot looking couple walking toward bar. She chose a short blue cocktail dress that matched my shirt perfectly, and wore a pair of silver fuck me heels.

We didn't know what door to go to when we arrived, so we chose the one with all the neon. When the door man saw us though, he said, "You guys here for the SDC party?"

I answered, "Yep."

"It's the door at the other end of the building."

"Oh, ok. Thanks man."

Once back outside, on our way to 'the other end', I said, "Do you think he was mad at me for calling him a man?"

We laughed together and were still smiling when we opened the other door and were greeted by another door man.

The music wasn't as loud as most clubs. We

couldn't see the club as we were in a rather small cloth box with the door man standing behind a podium. The door man said, "Good evening folks. Your SDC name?"

I glanced at Steph. I hadn't told her what the account name was. "Uh…Shehorny."

Steph just smiled.

The door man didn't blink an eye, just looked at his sheet of names. "Ah, here you are. Welcome. Have you been here before?"

"No."

"Ok, cool. I just need you to read and sign this release. It just says you are entering a place that may have some nudity, there are no pictures allowed, and there is no sex on the premises. If you would like to be added to our mailing list, you can put your email at the bottom."

I barely glanced at it and signed the bottom.

"You both need to sign it." He said to Steph.

"Oh, ok," she said and signed.

He continued, "It's $5 for guys with a lady, ladies are free, single guys are $10. Here is your wristband. This side of the building is exclusively for SDC members, although there is a back door that goes out onto the patio, and you can access the other club from their back door. No smoking inside our end, everyone goes out back. Here is a ticket for your first drink." He pulled back the black curtain that separated us from the bar, and with a bit of swagger in his voice, he said, "Have fun!"

I immediately noticed the lack of cigarette smoke. It was another thing Steph and I agreed on, smokers sucked. Who wants to kiss an ashtray?

The lighting wasn't as dark as our normal hang out, and the TV's didn't have sports playing. Writhing bodies, fucking, and pole dancers were the sport here. *Nice.*

I turned and took Steph's hand. She was looking around casually. We headed to the bar. It was just before 10 o'clock and there were about 30 people there. Just about every head turned our way when we came in. It was like the lions were waiting to see what was next up, on the menu.

I stopped before we got to the bar and asked Steph, "Where do you want to sit?"

She gestured with her chin toward the back side of the bar. I know she likes to see a place, and I can understand that. We wanted to be able to see what was going on for a while, before we interacted with the crowd.

I ordered us each a beer, and offered the one seat we found to Steph.

Steph looked to her right at a man that was standing in front of his seat. She looked back at me and took a drink. She asked me in a bar-whisper, "Do you want to sit? I don't think he is actually using his chair."

I waved it off nonchalantly. "No. No biggie.

I'm fine."

I think she was about to ask the guy if he would offer up his chair for me, when the guy actually beat her to the punch. "Hey, you guys want this chair? I never sit when I'm here."

Steph smiled, "Thank you so much." As he moved the chair more toward me she asked, "What's your name?" and stuck out her hand for a shake.

He turned her hand and instead kissed the back gently. "Erik. And you two are...?"

I reached out my hand hoping I would not get the same treatment. "Danny & Stephanie."

Thankfully, he shook it like a true man. He was strong and decisive about it, matching his stance. He was taller than me, and in similar, casual yet dressy, attire. "Do you come here often?" I paused and realized what that sounded like. "Wow it sounds pretty strange saying that to a guy."

"No problem. It's what we are here for right? Yes, I do come here often. Where are you guys from?"

We looked at each other and back to him. I said, "Here now. We moved here a short time ago. Just checkin' out the scene. Does it get busier, or is this the norm?"

"This is nothing yet. There's a big SDC party here tonight. It will be packed. The party officially started at nine when the doors open, although most of them don't come until around eleven."

Steph was looking at him with a bit more than just listening interest. She cocked her head a bit, and glanced at me with a raised eyebrow. I knew what that meant, she was giving the thumbs up for this to be 'The Guy.'

I looked back at Erik. He was looking over us at the crowd. He was a good foot taller than me and Steph sitting. "That's pretty late to get started. You always hang here that late?"

He smiled, "No. I like to roam around. If I find something to occupy me, I'll stay. If not…." He shrugged a shoulder.

Just then, a couple came around the other side of the bar. "Erik!" they said in unison. Both the woman and the man hugged Erik.

He replied, "Hey guys. Meet my friends Danny & Stephanie."

The woman said, "Well hello there. What a beautiful couple you are." She came over and gave Steph a hug, as if she'd known us forever.

Steph looked over at me from above the woman's shoulder. Not sure where this would lead, I decided to just sit back and watch the show.

Erik bought a round of drinks for everyone. I noticed he ordered a soda for himself. Not so usual chit chat went around since we all wanted to know who everyone was. Others joined our little circle at the back of the bar. We came to find out,

Erik was the hit of every party in town. He was starting to sound like me, when I was up north.

No one asked about what we did for a living. That is not something people share in places like this. The questions are almost always about sexual preferences, feeling out who wants what, and who is willing to do what.

Steph was catching a buzz and the music started to move her. She jumped up from her chair, and went to the dance floor. She is mesmerizing on the dance floor. I feel bad that I really don't like to dance, and she loves it.

I noticed Erik watching her, and he seemed to be moving to the beat as well.

I said, "Hey man, why don't you go dance with my woman. She would welcome a dance partner, and I never do."

He nodded his head to me, and went to the dance floor. He was a smooth operator, that's for sure. He knew how to dance, and had Steph laughing in minutes.

When they came back, Steph inquired, "So… Erik, would you consider coming home with us?" Her eyes flitted back and forth between us.

That's my girl. She says what she wants to say, no holding back.

"Sure." He looked at me, "You ok with that?"

"Absolutely. That's what we're here for, right?"

He nodded his head with a Touché smile.

Steph asked, "How do we do this? I mean, do we all just leave together and everyone knows?"

Erik answered, "You guys go out now. I have to settle up my tab and say good-bye. I'll be right out, then I'll follow you."

"Ok."

Steph looked at me. I turned to Erik and shook his hand again. I offered a hand to Steph, and we walked out to the car.

I turned the ignition off, as he pulled in the driveway behind us. I turned to Steph and said, "Okay. You can always say no to anything. Nothing is a sure thing. If you feel uncomfortable…"

She put a finger over my mouth momentarily, then followed it with her mouth. The kiss was warm and tasted of beer. "No worries. I'm your little nympho remember. I *have* done this before."

"Yeah. I know. I just don't want you to feel pressured or anything. This is all for us to have a heightened experience."

"It's all good. We better get out or he's gonna think we are freaking out or something." She opened her own door, and went to unlock the house.

Erik and I got out of our cars simultaneously.

He walked up to me, and shook my hand again. "Is this your first time?"

"Our first together. We each have done it before, with other people. She's a freak in the bed though, no worries there."

"Okay then."

He followed me in the house. Steph had turned on music, and lit some candles. *How do women do things so quickly?*

I led Erik to the living room just as Steph entered herself, wearing a short silk nighty. She wasn't wasting any time.

Erik smiled announcing, "Costume change!"

Steph sauntered over to me while I kicked off my shoes. She reached up and grabbed my head, pulling it down to her mouth, kissing me with lust. When she released me, she turned and looked at Erik. She didn't say anything, though I offered up, "Come on man join us."

Erik slipped off his own shoes. The two of us book ending her, I continued kissing her, and he came around the side of her neck and began caressing her lightly freckled skin with his lips.

Our hands became awkwardly intertwined around Steph's silky body. And before we knew it, just like in the porn, clothes were coming off. We were stripped down, our pants around our ankles. Steph sat down on the couch, I climbed up on the couch to let her suck my cock, and Erik went down to lick her pussy.

Steph's moans indicated full pleasure. I looked down to Erik and said, "Hey man, you need to stick your cock inside her, she really wants it.

"Anything you say."

He spit in his hand and rubbed it on the head of his cock, before inserting it into the open wetness he had created. With her mouth full to the brim on my own encouragement, a stifled exclamation of pleasure emitted from her.

He started slow at first. I could see her wetness glistening on his cock each time he pulled back. It made my own cock pulse with excitement. I was actually watching another man's cock fuck my woman. A live porno in my own living room. This is gonna make it hard for me, to hold off cumming.

I pulled out of Steph's mouth and stepped off the couch to give myself less stimulation, and to get a better view of the scene. I slowly stroked myself. Steph was really getting into it now. Erik had leaned in and really started pounding her. The sound of slapping ringing out, like the percussion section of the orchestra.

He looked up at me from his work, "You want some of this?"

"No. I am enjoying watching my woman as a porn star."

Steph said, "Yes, but I want to try DP."

Erik laughed. "Ah, so now I know why you wanted to bring me home." We all chuckled.

"Yes. We fuck like banshees. We watch a lot of porn, and she loves DP the most."

He finished a few more strokes. Then, like a jack-in-the-box, he quickly pulled out, and stood up. It must have felt pretty good, as Steph inhaled with pleasure.

Erik motioned to the couch. "You want me on the bottom or top?"

I looked at Steph. She motioned for me to sit, and when I did, she climbed on top of me. Her slick pussy glided easily over my all too hard shaft, she worked it a bit, before looking back at Erik for the invite.

He didn't need more than that. He moved between my legs and began directing his cock inside her.

Steph jerked up a bit. "No ass, I want to have you both in my pussy."

He readjusted his aim. Suddenly, it was my turn to flinch. I could feel the head of another man's cock pressing into my shaft. Something I never thought I would feel in my lifetime. I relaxed though. We had seen it in the movies, so it couldn't be all bad.

I literally felt the release of tension as her lips accepted his head, and suddenly, it was like her pussy became virginally tight. The tightness

The First Time

clamping down on me was intense.

I felt him slide up next to me. The sensations were unbelievable. Her softness and heat, mixed with ridges of him. Now I understood the 'ribbed for her pleasure' slogan. I was slightly embarrassed to admit just how much I was enjoying it.

Everything started slow, although, for only a brief amount of time. Erik sped up, and Steph's moans were escalating. She began gyrating her hips on me…and him. My cock was throbbing to cum. I had to hang on longer.

Erik adjusted his own legs to get a better stance and the pleasure escalated. I didn't know how it was possible to have this much stimulation. Erik started making noises, Steph was reaching her climax. This wasn't going to last long.

It began with Steph. "Oh yes! Baby I'm gonna cum!"

"Oh shit yeah! Cum for me Steph."

I could feel her pussy clench, the tightness was too much. Erik's momentum increased. "Oh God! Fuck!"

Erik's noises were much quieter, although I felt a warmth spread over my cock. Erik's last few strokes were frantic, buryied deep and hard.

Steph collapsed on me, shivering with aftershocks, as Erik pulled out.

"Which way is your bathroom?" I pointed, and he exited.

I said to Steph, "Oh my god babe. That was fucking amazing."

She only breathed, then kissed my neck in response.

"I never thought I was going to get off on a man's cock touching mine, but that was definitely part of what happened."

"Yes?"

"Your pussy was so fucking tight when he went in, and then I could feel him too. The whole ribbed thing… That was so intense. I can't even express how much, it was over the top."

"I do have to say, it was amazing on my end too. I was so filled. It was a lot, almost too much. Can we do it again?" There was a crazed sparkle in her eyes. I think I created an addict.

"I can't do anything right now babe, you know me. I need some time to recoup."

"No, I meant in the future. I don't need any more right now either. My pussy needs some recovery time."

"Oh, sure. You want Erik again, or someone new?"

"Doesn't matter. Just another cock will do." She smiled.

"That's my girl," I said, and kissed her on the nose. There may have been another man in the house, but for right now, all I could think about was me and my nympho.

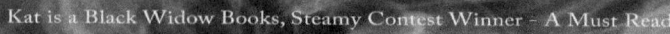

Seduced by 2

A Sexy Ménage à trois

MAYA LEARNS
BEST FRIENDS
SHARE ALL,
EVEN HER.

KAT CRIMSON

Seduced by 2

Kat Crimson

"Babe, is it alright? I told Foster he could come over later, for a few beers," Max asked in my ear, in a low, soothing voice. We were snuggled together on the couch watching a movie. His hand was absently stroking my arm. He must have felt me tense a bit at the mention of his friend's name, because he backpedalled. "I can call him back and tell him it's not a good night," he trailed off in a pseudo-question.

Foster was Max's amazingly beautiful best friend. The kind of male beauty that made him nearly blinding to look at – seriously, like weak in the knees, stammering, gibbering idiot beautiful. I could never relax when he was around. He made me anxious and self-conscious. It didn't even matter that he seemed like a really great guy, he just made me nervous. I felt guilty for my reaction. I loved Max so much. He was my life, but lord I had some impure thoughts about his best friend, really, really indecent thoughts.

"No babe, that's OK. Invite him over. You two never get to hang out. I feel like I'm monopolizing your time. I don't want to be that girlfriend… The one that steals you away and cuts you off from everyone who means something to you because I'm jealous of your time and your attention." I leaned into him, giving him a squeeze and a quick kiss. "Have a boy's night."

"Mai…Maya," began Max. "I want you to be there," he pleaded. He turned me to face him squarely, looking me in the eyes and giving my upper arms a soft squeeze. "Foster's my best friend and I feel like you two don't get along, or like you avoid him for some reason. You two are my favorite people in the universe. I want – no I need – you to get along with each other."

Panic. How was I supposed to interact and function while Foster was around? Just the sight of him brought a blush to my cheeks and instantly made naughty thoughts pop into my head. It made me feel so awful and so guilty, and I definitely didn't want Max to see that. He didn't deserve that. I would have to find a way; it clearly meant so much to Max. I had to do it.

I pasted a smile on my face, though inside I

was quaking. "Great," I said. If Max could sense the falseness in my overenthusiastic tone, he didn't let on. "That sounds great. I can't wait."

I am going to hell. I gave Max my best innocent doe eyes. He leaned in with a smile and gave me a deep, lingering kiss that soothed my frayed nerves and made my body begin to tingle. He pulled away just as I wanted him to claim much more, then came the sound of the doorbell and the front door being pushed open.

"Hello?" A deep, melodic, voice sounded from the front of the house. "Is everybody decent?"

Not nearly, I thought as my nipples perked up and the blood slowly pooled to my clit at the sound of his voice. Foster's beautiful voice. He was the singer and lead guitarist in a local band that was doing pretty well. They had a fairly big following – it wasn't all horny girls either - they were actually good, in a dark, indie rock sort of way that reminded me a bit of Interpol, or maybe Echo and the Bunnymen.

My palms went sweaty and my mouth a bit dry as he found us in the living room. He popped his head in with a wide, charismatic, grin. "What's up kids?"

"Hey Foster," Max smiled back, waving him in. "Long time no see, buddy, what's n—oooh, beer!" Max broke off mid-thought, mesmerized by the drinks, "and whiskey too!! Good man!" grinned Max.

"Yeah, I brought a few refreshments," Foster affirmed, then sat down right next to me on the couch.

Gulp, I was now sandwiched between Max and Foster. "Hi Foster," I said a bit shyly. "Good to see you again."

"Good to be seen," Foster said, surprising me by leaning in to give me a friendly kiss on the cheek. My hand reflexively came up to rest on his ribcage.

Sweet Jesus, I think I'm in shock! I blinked as the realization that Foster's lips had just touched my cheek hit my brain. And holy fuck! His flesh felt fantastic – even through the fabric of his tee – I could feel the supple, corded muscle. It was a struggle not to slide my hand along it. I pulled my hand back quickly, taking a shaky breath and scootching into Max a bit.

"How about a shot, pretty Maya?" asked Foster, twisting the cap off a fresh bottle of nice Irish whiskey.

"Umm, sure," I replied, biting my lip a bit nervously. Foster slid the mouth of the bottle towards my lips as if to pour a shot into my mouth. He must have seen my quizzical expression, because he winked at me and said, "We're all friends here." Just as Max also said, "No need to waste glasses."

I hesitantly opened my mouth as Max placed a kiss at my temple and rubbed my arms reassuringly from behind. I think he could tell this was making me nervous.

The bottle gently touched my lips and Foster tilted it up, pouring the searing liquid into my mouth. It was too much. I had to close my lips to swallow before it started overflowing. I gulped it down, coughing lightly spilling some down my jaw as Foster pulled the bottle away.

"Oops, sorry Maya." Foster grinned as his free hand shot out to wipe the excess off my face, his thumb slid over my jaw, just as the burn of the whiskey hit my belly turning my insides molten. He lifted his thumb to his full sensuous lips and sucked the whiskey off of it.

What the fuck??? I think my brain is about to short circuit from the sight of that. I can't believe he just did that in front of Max. What the hell is going on?

"Give it here," demanded Max, holding his hand out to Foster for the bottle.

Foster took a swig first. His tongue slid out to lick the top of the bottle as his eyes met mine, before setting his lips over it, tilting his head back and taking a healthy swig. I felt like flames were licking my insides. I could feel my cheeks heat up. Why was he playing with me like this? And with Max right there?

Foster handed the bottle over to Max leaning in closely over my body as he did so, and placing a hand on my shoulder for balance…and my god did he smell good. I could feel the outline of each individual finger on my shoulder where his hand practically singed my flesh.

"I brought a movie over," Foster said sitting back up straight, his hand still burning a hole through my shoulder. "I think you guys will like it," he chuckled a bit. "It's got a killer soundtrack." Foster got up and walked over to the DVD player, and I tried – and failed miserably – not to look at his tight, firm ass, encased in worn but well-fitting jeans.

I snapped out of my misbehavior when Max held the whiskey in front of me and said, "Take another swig Mai." I needed it. I took the bottle from Max and downed a good sized portion of whiskey, just as Foster finished inserting the movie and came back over to the couch.

He reached out for the bottle of whiskey and I handed it to him. His fingers slid over mine as he took it from me, a small smirk sliding over his features. "Somebody's messy," he said, and I could not look away as his tongue came out to swipe the side of the bottle, licking the dripping whiskey from it. My eyes flew to his throat to watch him swallow as he poured another shot down his throat.

Foster leaned back over me again to give the bottle back to Max. He cracked a couple beers, handed one to me, then sat back, closer than before… too close. I could feel the heat and electricity emanating from his body. I was so nervous that I was trembling, and my breathing was becoming erratic. I needed to get my shit together. Being this close to Foster, and his odd flirting, was really disconcerting.

"What's a matter babe?" asked Max in a solicitous tone. "Are you cold?" he asked pulling me back against his chest and sliding his hot hands up and down my arms. "Why don't you put your feet up?" he continued without giving me a chance to answer. "Foster will rub your feet. It's fine," he said, sensing my hesitation he added "Foster gives amazing foot rubs– don't you buddy?"

In answer, Foster reached down to grab my feet and pull them into his lap, sliding his beautiful guitarist's hands over my sock clad feet.

I chugged on my beer, hoping it would provide me with some liquid courage.

Foster's gaze scanned the room and came to rest on a bottle of lotion sitting on the coffee table. "Ah," he exclaimed, reaching out for it, then dropping it on the couch next to him before sliding my socks off. His hands slipped under the hem of my pants searching for the tops of my socks. He cocked a brow at me quizzically when he was unsuccessful.

I giggled. Giggled? Wow, the alcohol must

be hitting me pretty fast. I hadn't had much to eat today. Foster's nimble fingers began sliding my pants legs up, and up, and up. I had over-the-knee socks on, a luxurious cashmere argyle. His hands stroked over them. I saw his eyes widen slightly. I think Foster was a fan of my socks…

He shifted in his seat, settling the arch of my foot over his hard groin. It caused me to catch my breath in nervous shock, and avert my gaze. He reverently began to peel the socks down my calves as if nothing was out of the ordinary. "Those are some great socks," he said, pulling them off of my feet and running his fingers over my smooth legs – thank god I'd shaved.

"I'll start the movie," Max said, pausing the hands that were still sliding over my arms long enough to grab the remote and press play. "What are we watching?" he asked Foster as his hands moved to my shoulders, rubbing the tension out of them.

"It's called '9 Songs'," replied Foster as he rubbed lotion into his palms. "It's kind of an art-house porn," he admitted sheepishly. "But the live bands and the songs make the movie brilliant." I felt his lotion covered hands slide over my sensitive feet. I gasped at the ticklish contact, trying not to kick. I took another large swig of my beer.

"Is somebody ticklish?" asked Foster with a wicked grin, as he slid a fingertip up the middle of the bottom of my foot. My foot shot out involuntarily, catching him solidly in the thigh, as I let out a screech.

Max chuckled behind me as he devilishly poked his fingers into my armpits and began to torture me. I was screaming for them to stop, flailing my arms and kicking my feet, completely out of control, and laughing. "Stop! Stop! Stop! Please!!" I begged them. My belly started to ache from laughter as they grabbed for my flailing limbs, trying to keep me from hitting anything vital.

Foster had a grip on my legs. He slid between my thighs to avoid my kicking feet. Max had my arms now gripped and held in place behind my body. On the television screen a couple was full on going at it in passionate abandon. The moans and sex sounds permeated the living room. I realized that the grip Max had on my arms was thrusting my breasts out for Foster's hungry gaze. My clothing had become displaced in the scuffle, and my cleavage was borderline indecent.

I felt Max's hard cock pressing against the small of my back. His lips came down on my neck in an open mouthed kiss. Foster's stare remained locked on my breasts. Still in his strong grasp, I felt his thumbs slowly, tracing circles on my thighs. I shivered with lust, trapped between two sexy men, restrained by their powerful, yet gentle hands. The hot fucking going on in the corner of the room, where the DVD played, made for a moment that was pregnant with sexual tension. We were on the precipice of something. I wanted this something to happen. I hadn't been this turned on in… ever.

Max's hands slipped over my arms, releasing them so he could cup my breasts. He squeezed them together, nearly forcing them to spill out over the low neck of my shirt displaying them to even better advantage for Foster.

Foster groaned and slid his hands to the backs of my thighs, gripping and pulling my lower body into him, pulling my center up to meet his straining erection.

Oh my fucking god!

His hands continued, traveling up the back of my thighs. Suddenly, my ass was gripped tightly in his large palms and he was sliding the wet, clothing covered seam of my sex, up and down his thick, jeans covered shaft. I moaned in something that resembled pleasure, but was really much more primal. An incendiary heat was overtaking my core.

My brain was fogged with lust. Many strange thoughts swirled hazily and sluggishly through the dense, molten rivers of pleasure. Had they done this before? Had Max and Foster always shared their girlfriends? Or was this something new? Was I the first? Why? As Max gently bit into the side of my neck, temporarily short circuiting my brain and derailing the few thoughts I was able to form. Fuck it! I thought, who cares?

His thumbs and forefingers were squeezing my nipples tightly. The pressure increased gradually, sending torturous jolts of current through my throbbing cunt. When he reached my threshold – where pleasure turns to pain – he held the pressure steady. He skirted and flirted with that edge so delicately and perfectly. Max knows my body so well. Sometimes I feel like I am his puppet.

"I want to watch you suck Foster's cock Maya," Max said in a tone that was part plea, but mostly a demand. The demand portion was something new. He wasn't usually forceful with me. He preferred to get his way through subtle manipulation and with a heavy application of his undeniable charm. I was incredibly turned on by this new tone.

"Unzip my pants Maya," Foster pleaded in a dramatic, frantic voice, which made it sound like he thought he might actually die if I didn't comply immediately. His words were punctuated by an extra hard squeeze to my ass cheeks as he pulled my body in even harder, and he let out a harsh groan, closing his eyes in agony.

"Do it Maya," whispered Max in my ear. "Unzip Foster, and pull his cock out. Now." Max whispered this command in a calm, hot voice, just before biting my ear lobe and tugging it with his teeth as his tongue lightly licked and rubbed over it.

I don't have the words to tell you what that softly delivered directive did to my insides, but outside my hands lifted shakily towards the zipper of Foster's jeans. With trembling fingers, I skimmed my hand over the sizeable bulge in Foster's pants. I undid his top button, took hold of the zipper tab, and pulled. It was such a deafening sound. It was as if everyone had been holding their collective breath, in anticipation, and perhaps we all had. Even the movie had momentarily gone quiet. Then one of the songs came on, just as I slipped my hand inside to grasp Foster's hot, velvety cock, it was 'C'mon, C'mon' by the Von Bondies. Even the movie was impatient with me…

As I slid my fingers down the thick length of Foster's cock, trying to find the end of it so I could gently pull him out, my eyebrows rose and my eyes went round. Foster was a big, big boy. When I glanced shyly up at his delicious face, that look he usually wore, like there was a joke you weren't privy to, was completely gone. He was moaning and looking down at me like I was some sort of angel of mercy, as I finally pried him from his pants.

Holy shit! I had definitely never taken anything that large, in my mouth or elsewhere…

It was intimidating yet it was an incredibly thrilling turn-on. Suddenly I couldn't wait until he fought his way inside of my tight channel and my body was forced to accommodate him. Max was by no means small, but Foster...

As Foster slowly eased me off of his lap, Max began to murmur in my ear, calmly explaining, in very few words, exactly how things were going to go. "Foster is going to fuck your cunt, and I'm going to fuck your ass Maya." It was as plain as that. It was black and white. It was inescapable.

As he said it, one of his hands discontinued its torment of my breast and slid down my abdomen, delving into my waistband. He slipped it underneath my panties, and then slid his fingers through my slick folds, and inserted two.

I moaned and closed my eyes as he penetrated me. I was thinking about those impossibly hot images in my mind. I'd never been with two men at once. I'd fantasized about it plenty. I'd even fantasized about Max and Foster. Something told me that those fantasies wouldn't even come close...

I reopened my eyes to find the tip of Foster's beautiful cock staring me in the face as he kneeled in front of me. He gripped his massive shaft, aiming it towards my parted mouth. I stole another glance at him. He was looking at my mouth with a feral intensity that made me lick my lips in anticipation. He let out a strangled breath and brought the head of his cock, already leaking a shimmering clear bead of precum, to rest on my moist lips.

It wasn't even a conscious thought, my tongue just darted out of my mouth to swipe that tiny bead of clear fluid from the tip, then darted right back in so I could savor that small taste of him.

He let out a growl and gripped the back of my neck, holding my head firmly in place, as he used his other hand to guide his cock around the opening of my mouth, painting my lips with the steady stream of fluid leaking out of him. When my tongue swept out again, and my breath skated over his cock, he let out a tortured groan and began to feed his thick length into my mouth.

"Fuck Maya," he groaned out. "You have no idea how many times I've thought about having that, pretty mouth of yours stretched over my cock. Suck me Maya. Suck on my cock," he pleaded as his fingers made small, persuasive circles in the hair at the nape of my neck. My mouth eased open wider and his hips slid forward filling and stretching my mouth with his velvety yet hard shaft. I began to suck.

Foster let out the most amazing sound of pleasure. I never wanted to stop hearing that sound. It made me feel so good to know that I could bring him so much pleasure, so I sucked even harder. I forced myself to take even more of his thick length, wanting to give him even more pleasure. I began to get lost in the desire to please Foster. I felt Max's fingers, which had stilled inside my body, begin to move again. A groan forced its way out of my throat. It swept through Foster. His eyes nearly rolled back as he gripped my neck hard. Max murmured against my neck, just below my ear, "that is the most erotic thing I've seen in my life Mai."

Max's fingers moved slowly in and out of my wet pussy, sliding his thumb rhythmically over my clit in a hypnotic movement that some-how managed to direct my mouth up and down Foster's shaft. We were totally in sync. It was the most in tune I'd ever felt in my life, like we were a set of instruments all playing each other.

"Watching you suck Foster's cock makes me want to tear your clothes off with my teeth Mai," Max growled into my ear before giving my lobe a nip. "It makes me want to slam my cock into your tight cunt and fuck you senseless," he ground out, thrusting into my cunt with a third finger. He drove it as deep and hard as he could and held it there, applying all of that delicious pressure while his hips bucked and he ground his hard cock into my fleshy ass.

I moaned at his words, and at the feel of his fingers forcing their way in, and taking hold of something more than my insides, something deeper and more powerful.

Foster let out a strangled groan. He was losing control and he was powerless to do anything to stop it. He thrust harder than before, making me gag and choke on his shaft. His arm was trembling, like he was fighting with himself over pulling out or pushing in deeper.

My eyes were tearing up, and I couldn't breathe, but I stayed calm. I fought to control my urge to gag and cough. Foster held his cock there, lodged deep inside my mouth, teasing my throat, stretching my lips and jaw wide, (barely half-way in), for another few seconds before beginning to withdraw.

"You're so fucking beautiful Mai," Max whispered in my ear. His fingers slowed to a tender rhythm within my body. He began to kiss and lick and suck my neck reverently. "I love you so much, you're so amazing," he finished as his cock slid against the valley of my ass in soft, soothing up and down motions.

"I can't take any more of your mouth Maya," Foster confessed. "I'm going to lose it if you so much as breathe on me." He pulled all the way out then, sliding his hands delicately up my arms to my shoulders, pushing me upright so he could kiss my lips, hungrily, yet tenderly. Foster held me in placed as his mouth wandered all over my lips and cheeks and chin, my nose, my eyelids, making love to my face with his beautiful mouth.

I felt so cherished, sandwiched between these two amazing men who were treating my body like it was the most precious thing on this earth.

Foster continued using his mouth to turn me into a weak and needy bundle of desire. He slid his tongue down my neck, so there was now a mouth fastened to either side of my throat. It was so incredible.

In unison, Max and Foster began to slide my clothes from my body, peeling away my shirt, unbuttoning and unzipping my pants, lifting and maneuvering my limbs like experts. They slid my pants down my legs and off without stopping the movements of their lips across my electrically charged flesh.

My socks were gone and I was down to just my sheer, petal pink, lacy underwear set. At that point, both men sat back and drank in the sight of me.

Men are so easily enthralled by girls in underwear.

That thought crept randomly into my lust and whiskey addled brain, causing me to giggle and bite my lip. Foster grinned at me as his hands crept towards my chest and his fingers slid slowly and gently over my taut breasts for the first time. His thumbs played with my nipples, making me gasp. His grin widened. It was devastating. It was consuming!

Max's hands moved to my hips and pulled me gently back onto his body until I was sitting on his lap. Foster's body followed mine keeping contact with my flesh, teasing me the whole time, that amazingly sexy grin on his face. I couldn't look away if I wanted to.

"Take your panties off!" Max ordered.

Max's voice sent a jolt of lust through the parts that were soon to be unveiled. My hands raced to do his bidding. I lifted my hips as I rolled the sides of my lacy undies over my curves. The pool of damp arousal coating them caused them to stick to my folds as I peeled them from my body. I ground my ass into Max's cock as I leaned forward to slide them down and off my legs. Foster's hands momentarily left my breasts as he looked on with lust.

Max's hands found the clasp of my bra as I started to sit back up in his lap. His agile fingers making short work of the disconnection process. My heavy breasts gratefully springing back to their natural position as the elastic released them from their tightly constricted confines. Max began sliding the straps down my arms, halting midway down my bicep so that Foster could take over. Foster grasped my straps from the other side and finished pulling them down, exposing my naked breasts to his hungry gaze. Foster immediately leaned forward to take my hard nipple between lips and we groaned, simultaneously, as soon as his mouth settled over my flesh.

Max's hands settled on my inner thighs and traced the outline of my groin to either side of my aching cunt, where my thighs met my hips. Meeting in the center, one of his hands slid over my clit and the other moved to my needy hole. I gasped in pleasure as he worked my cunt like a master and pulled back on my body to press me harder against his rigid cock, sandwiched between the rounded globes of my two ass cheeks.

Foster was kneeling on the couch in front of me sitting back on his folded knees, which were between my own parted ones. He moved his hands all over my breasts, then lifted his face back to mine so he could attack my mouth with a hard, hungry kiss. His hands move down my sides, and slipped around my ass as he continued to melt my brain with the heat of his kiss.

Max's hands were still wreaking havoc on my lower regions, manipulating my clit and fucking my sex with his beautiful, long, artistic fingers. I moaned into Foster's kiss as Max's hands demanded a response from me, then gasped, as suddenly Foster's grip on my ass became hard and he lifted me from Max's lap into his own. Max's fingers slid out of me as he did this, but they were replaced by the feel of my hot, slick cunt gliding down the impossible length and girth of Foster's massive erection. My folds parted to wrap around and lubricate his cock as he slid it along my sex without trying to penetrate, just to tease. I wanted him inside of me. Now!

"It's time Maya," whispered Max in my ear as he shimmied back up to my body, plastering himself, once again, to my backside. "Foster is going to fuck your sweet pussy now," he continued. "Don't worry, Mai, he's totally clean. We would never put you in any danger that way," Max reassured.

Holy fuck!!! With all that had happened tonight... the novelty of it all, and the hard liquor carelessly tossed down... I hadn't even thought... I mean, the thought that Foster's bare, uncovered cock was about to find a home inside of my wet, unprotected sex... it never even entered my head. I was so in lust right now, I hadn't – I couldn't - even think. I was mindless with need. Of course I was on the pill. Max and I had been together and monogamous for a while, we trusted each other. It had just gone there naturally as we both craved, so much, to be closer and to remove any barriers that were hindering that.

I needed to say something I realized. No matter how much in need we all were, I don't think they would have continued without me saying, "I trust you. I trust you both." Max's arms came around to hug me fiercely as I said those words and Foster's mouth crashed down on mine once more as I felt him guide his tip, which was oozing pre-cum, to my entrance.

"We'll take it slow, Maya," Foster breathed into my lips. "I don't want to tear you up," he said, then kissed me gently and began to nibble on my lips as he started to feed the tip into me. I gasped and he groaned as if he was in pain, gripping my ass hard. He was almost panting when he admitted, "I want so badly to drive myself deep inside of you, to the hilt, and take you completely in one swift, hard stroke."

His words sent a fresh flood of moisture to coat his invading member, as I moaned into his mouth. One part of me wanting him to do it, to just drive himself in deep and take me hard. The other part realizing that he would rip me right in half if he did that. His slow progress was already making me wince in pain and causing sweat to break out as I gritted my teeth against the stretching that was starting to feel almost like tearing.

He backed off a bit, then started a series of shallow fucks. His cock getting coated in my juices and making a tiny bit more progress on each inward thrust, stretching me a bit more, but never crossing that very thin line between pleasure and hideous pain. He was walking a tightly controlled knife's edge, and - fuck - it felt so amazing! I couldn't wait to be able to take him all. I wanted him to be able to let go within me and fuck me hard. Something told me we'd need to do this a lot more if my body were ever to become accustomed to his enough to be able to do that. I very much hoped it came to pass. Not even finished with our first time and already I was hooked.

"God Mai, you're doing so well. You're taking his cock so beautifully. You have no idea how incredible you are to watch, and how much it turns me on to see your sweet cunt stretched wide to swallow up my best friend's massive cock," Max said placing feather light kisses along my temple and cheek. "I love you so much, your trust, your lust, your insatiable hunger for exploration."

His words were making me glow, and I turned my head in need, seeking his mouth for a deep, passionate kiss as his hands came up to play, gently, lovingly with my breasts. He caressed them as we kissed, and Foster continued to penetrate my body with his huge cock. Max's tender care was soothing and distracting me from any of the pain of Foster's entrance.

"That's it Maya," Foster breathed into my ear. "Take my cock, take every inch of it. I'm going to fuck you like you've never been fucked before," he promised. "I'm going to fill you more than you've ever been filled," His coarse words caused the muscles of my pussy to involuntarily clench around his cock, making him groan in my ear and grip me even harder. "Fuck Mai!" he exclaimed. "You're absolutely killing me. You have the sweetest, tightest pussy I think I've ever been in, and I want to fuck it so hard." He groaned again, his hips thrusting in another quick inch, before he forced himself to slow down upon hearing my swift intake of breath, almost like an indrawn scream.

That had hurt…not unbearably, but it was definitely painful…and also exhilarating and amazing, making me feel so gloriously full. I knew that when I came on Foster's cock, which was inevitable, it was going to be a monumental orgasm.

Foster came to a halt. He was completely still inside of me now, waiting for me to adjust, and to let the tight grip of my cunt relax. His breath was harsh in my ear, and I could tell he was holding himself in check. Max's hands had also stilled, his thumbs and forefingers were applying constant, hard pressure to my nipples though. It was sending sparks to my clit, causing the blood to throb and pulse through my cunt.

Max started to rub his cock up and down in the valley of my ass. He kissed my nape and murmured encouragements into my flesh that were too soft to hear. He always undid me with the way he understood my body so well, like he was inside my head and could see exactly what I needed and when I needed it.

It was amazing having one man inside of me and the other behind me, knowing he would also be inside of me soon, having their mouths and their hands all over my body, having them utter filthy, naughty and incredibly sweet things in my ears. As my mind wandered over how amazing this all was Foster slid in another slow inch. My breath stilled. I looked down to see that he was about three quarters of the way in. I'd never been so stuffed with cock in all of my life. I felt like he'd already hit the end of me. I could feel his tip rubbing along my cervix in an oddly pleasurable, yet somewhat uncomfortable caress. I watched in amazement as my cunt continued to expand and to swallow his cock, not sure how I would fit the rest in, or where it would go.

Foster's forehead came down to rest on mine as he continued applying pressure. He pushed forward with his thick cock, trying to get more of it inside of me. My teeth found his shoulder as he began, again, to make shallow thrusts. I was riding that edge even more intensely now... Pleasure or pain? As the thick, raised veins of Foster's meaty cock rubbed along my insides it became an intense pleasure. I could feel an orgasm building swiftly. It was such a surprise, because it hadn't been that slow building of pleasure like it was with Max.

Max reacted to every breath and movement and gasp I made, and took advantage of it to cause me the most pleasure. With Foster it hadn't really even been all that pleasurable as he pushed into me, it had mostly been slow, uncomfortable and nearly painful. Something changed now as his shallow, filling strokes began to find a rhythm, and he was able to get most of his cock inside of me to press on all sorts of delicious spots that hadn't ever been pressed like this before.

All of a sudden my cunt was nearly burning with the need to explode in orgasm. My pussy was so stretched and it felt like Foster was pummeling into my bladder, or something. I needed to cum, or to pee, I couldn't tell which? It felt crazy and amazing and…

Suddenly, Foster pulled his cock completely out of me. I screamed as my entire body convulsed, and liquid began gushing out in forceful squirts all over Foster's rock hard cock, abdomen, and thighs.

Holy shit! I am squirting! This is what it feels like to squirt! Sweet mother fuck! This is bloody amazing! I thought as my body shook. Foster looked on with a huge, cocky grin, and Max gripped me tightly, practically making out with my ear lobe.

"You're fucking amazing Maya," Foster said, just as I felt Max slide his dick between my thighs to soak up some of the moisture flowing freely from my sensitive cunt. My body struggled in Max's grip, trying not to let my pussy be touched, but Max was very firm with me as his cock teased my sensitive folds, making me cry out and tremble.

"I'm so hard right now Mai," Max growled in my ear. "Your ass is mine," he threatened.

As he said those possessive words to me, I felt the head of his cock slide back through my folds. He punched his cock up into my cunt once, with brutal force, burying himself to the hilt and making my body go rigid. I uttered one shattered groan as his cock forced my sensitive flesh to wrap around it and feel things it wasn't quite ready to yet. My body shuddered uncontrollably as it tried to handle the sensations and it was both a sweet torture and a relief as he pulled out.

"Mine," he whispered in my ear, "it's still mine," he said. "You are still mine." I nearly came again at his words. The tip of his cock left my entrance and made its way backwards up to the tightly puckered flesh of my asshole.

"You're going to cum again, Mai, as I fuck your ass." promised Max in a gritty, low voice. "And when you're cumming from my rock hard cock riding your ass into submission," he continued, while I shivered in lust at his domineering words, "Foster is going to shove his big fat dick back inside your tight little slit. Together we are going to fill you up and fuck you raw."

Holy fuck!

I gasped and shivered at the pure jolt of lust his words sent coursing through my body. Just then I felt the tip of his cock, still slick from bathing in my juices, begin to press on the tight ring of flesh between my ass cheeks. It made me groan as he slowly forced his way inside.

Max's arm crept around me, pulling my body back tightly against his. My breast was mashed against his strong bicep as his hand came down to cup my entire sex and slide over it in slow massaging circles that had loosened the clenched muscles of my aching cunt, as well as my asshole. Max pressed his advantage, sliding his big, hard dick deeply inside of my ass. I gasped with the intrusion.

Though not nearly as large as Foster's, Max's cock was still quite big, and definitely a struggle to take in my ass. If Max hadn't been training me with plugs, and using his fingers and tongue on me on a continual basis, I don't think I ever could have taken him there. I was so aroused right now though, that my ass was practically begging to be claimed. I couldn't wait to feel two cocks inside of me at once. It would be the first time for me. I felt my back arch, on its own, as my body pushed itself down on him, trying to take him completely inside. I was so turned on that I barely felt any discomfort at all. It would normally take quite a bit of foreplay and teasing and warm up to reach this state where I could take Max's entire thick length in my backside and feel only pleasure, yet tonight my body was on fire. I needed it there. I needed more.

"That's it Maya, take it all." encouraged Max in a ragged, low moan. "Take it deep." he ordered. He groaned as my tight asshole clenched down on him in reaction to his words. He began to mutter almost incoherently as his cock started to move in me, and he slipped his fingers inside of my soaked sex, rubbing his thumb over my clit. "I'm gonna fuck that tight ass so hard Mai... Fuck! ...so good...feels so good babe... gonna make you scream." His promise came on a grunt, as his dick slammed inside of my ass, balls deep. My breath whooshed out on a panting, half scream, half moan of tortured pleasure.

I watched through half lidded eyes, glazed and slitted with pleasure, as Foster knelt in front of me. Foster watched Max take my ass from behind, making my breasts jiggle, watching the fingers of Max's hand disappearing inside of me and reappearing, listening to his best friend utter filthy words in my ear as I moaned in need and in pleasure. He was stroking his rigid cock to us, panting with lust at the sight before him, just waiting for the right moment to join in, and holding himself in check until then.

Max's cock was thrusting in and out of my ass in long, strong, strokes. He was truly fucking my ass hard, just as he'd promised, and it felt fucking marvelous. He'd never been this rough with my ass before. He was gripping my body and my sex so tightly. I felt like he was the only thing holding me together, that if he let go I would fly apart into a million pieces. As tightly as he held onto me, I wanted him to hold even more tightly, to fuck me even more deeply and furiously, until whatever this thing I felt reaching up through me, with so much force, erupted, and we shattered with it.

I could feel every taut, hard, sweat-slicked inch of Max's body against my back, sliding and slapping into me with every thrust. We panted and moaned and grunted in unison as Foster madly stroked his cock, his pre-cum dripping everywhere.

Max fastened his lips to the side of my neck, sucking on the sensitive flesh where the hot pulsing blood flows north and south just under the surface of my smooth skin. He brought a hand to my throat, gently squeezing as his other hand hooked into my sex and levered back on it fiercely, as he thrust inside of my ass like a frenzied beast, taking me so hard my entire body started to tremble. We both began to scream at the exact same time as his hot cum started to flood my asshole and I began to gush all over his fingers. Max bit my neck as I orgasmed. It made me cum even harder, as did the hand he pulled from my grasping cunt as he began to lightly slap my wet pussy with it, nearly making me black out in pleasure.

I was so far gone I almost didn't see as Foster slapped Max's hand aside in his frenzy to get his cock back inside of me. I was not so far gone that I didn't notice when he started pushing it in though. Oh my fuck!

Despite Max having just cum inside of my ass, he was still hard. It was a gift of his, he could stay hard and ready for hours and hours, regardless of how many times he came. It was a perfect foil for my insatiably greedy pussy. It wasn't why I loved him so much, although it certainly didn't hurt.

Foster pushed inside my hyper sensitive and utterly soaked pussy with his massive and incredibly stiff cock. I could feel them both inside of me, meeting and sliding along opposite sides of the same barrier. It made the aftershocks of my wild orgasm even more powerful. I trembled between Max and Foster, completely overwhelmed by the feeling of the two men's cocks dueling inside of me. They filled me like nothing I'd ever felt before and caused sensations inside of me I had no words to describe, other than pure bliss.

My head lolled to the side and I was panting heavily as Max's cock remained buried in me, to the hilt, and Foster was still sliding in slowly. At last, Foster's balls rested squarely against the flesh of my dripping cunt; both men lodged inside of me as far and as deep as they could get, and not moving. The only movement was our straining breaths, and the blood pounding through our veins.

The movie had ended and the only sounds that could be heard were the ragged breaths and mingled moans of our three joined bodies becoming one.

This moment was unspeakably beautiful and will be etched in my brain until the day I cease to breath.

I could tell we all felt it.

Foster's mouth came down over mine as swiftly as a striking adder, yet he kissed me with deadly gentleness. He stole my breath away as both of Max's hands moved between us to cup my full breasts, and he began to make love to the flesh of my shoulder, neck and nape with his mouth. Max was breathing sweet, unintelligible, inaudible words into my nape, which sent shivers down my spine, causing the muscles in my ass, my thighs, and between my legs, to tighten and clutch at their buried flesh.

I whimpered into Foster's sweet, beautiful kiss as they both began to fight the grasp of my body by moving within me, forcing me to loosen my stranglehold on their cocks. It only caused my flesh to grip more tightly.

Max bit down on my shoulder in tortured agony and Foster groaned into my mouth. They both began to fuck me harder, one fucking into me as the other pulled out, and vice versa. I cannot begin to describe the feeling of their opposing cocks sliding in and out of both of my holes at the same time. Sounds I had never made before and cannot even try to describe were coming out of my throat. Both Foster and Max were making noises of their own, that I'll just call 'extreme pleasure'.

Then, suddenly, Max pulled out of my ass completely and I uttered a bereft moan at the loss of his cock. Foster wrapped his arms tightly around me and kissed me deeply while he continued to fill me with his thick thrusting shaft. He embedded himself deeply, only pulling out a few inches before thrusting back in, preferring to stay mostly buried while he fucked my sweet sex.

"Bedroom," barked Max, in the grips of a powerful, lust driven need. "I want Maya to ride my face, on all fours, as you take her pussy from behind...doggy style." He directed his comments to Foster, but the effect they had on my own brain, as I listened to what he wanted, nearly made me short circuit. I would have come again on Foster's cock, right then and there, if Foster hadn't stopped moving. He lifted my legs up to wrap around his waist, as he stood up from the couch to comply.

I almost came anyway when Max gripped the back of Foster's neck and pulled him in for a passionate kiss as I lay sandwiched between the two men. My breath came hard and my pussy began rhythmically milking Foster's fully embedded flesh.

Max broke the kiss off and Foster moaned in loss, as Max said, "Don't you dare Mai, don't you even think about cumming yet," he ordered with a hiss.

So busted. I let out a frustrated moan as I struggled to force my orgasm back down. What I had just been witness to, along with all that we'd done together this night, was making it very difficult to have any composure whatsoever. I felt completely out of control, and it was utterly, fucking fantastic.

"No Maya," Max ordered. He gripped my face between both hands, as he forced me to look him in the eyes, "You will not come again until you are on all fours, for Foster's cock, and I am laying beneath that sweet pussy, sucking on your clit, as you ride my face." I began to shake in need and in panic.

Did he think those words, and the look of pure need and lust and total domination that he was aggressively forcing me to witness were going to stave off my need to explode in orgasm? Because they were having the exact opposite effect. I have never wanted to cum so badly in my entire life, and I have never tried to hold back my orgasm before. I always take my pleasure as it comes. My entire body was shaking with this new effort of holding back my pleasure, and as Foster began to walk towards the bedroom, I nearly broke.

"Don't!" I begged him, "Please don't move yet Foster." I nearly sobbed, my pussy throbbing and clutching at his shaft, as my arms wrapped tightly around his shoulders and back, clutching him hard, as I tried to focus on my breathing. Foster began to sooth me with a hand on my back and whispered words in my ear.

"Shhh, Maya. It's okay," he lulled me. "It'll pass," he continued to sooth, "…just breathe slow and deep."

He continued his soothing movements on my back as he began to walk again, into the bedroom, never ceasing his steady stream of encouraging words. Before I knew it, we were at the king-size bed. Max was already lying in wait, his body was stretched perpendicularly across the bed, face-up, with his head close to the edge. Foster's thighs met the sides and he began to let me slip from his arms onto the bed. I clutched at him, not wanting to let go of the intimate contact.

"Sixty-nine, Mai," urged Max. "I need to feel your lips around my aching hard cock as Foster fucks you more deeply than you have ever been fucked before," he continued in agonized lust. I could see how hard and how red he was, as I watched the pre-cum oozing from his tortured tip. I wanted to taste it, I wanted to ease his need and soothe his aching flesh with my mouth. I needed it as badly as he did.

"I want to feel how the reaction reaches your mouth, as Foster buries himself in you until you feel like you can't possibly take any more." Max admitted in complete abandon, overtaken by his lustful visions. "I want to feel it when he pushes you beyond that point and turns you into a wild animal, forcing you to take everything he gives you as he fucks you with his massive tool, turning you into a greedy slave to his cock. I want to feel your mouth engulf my cock as I fuck your face and claim your virgin throat Maya."

I don't know if Max had any idea of the effect of his words on me. I almost didn't need Foster's cock at all. I was already turning into a wild animal from just his words and the images they put in my head. I could tell that Foster was also not unaffected, as his cock pulsed and jerked inside of me just before he slid it out on a tortured grunt.

I scrambled on the bed, hastily straddling Max and sliding a hand over his balls, cupping them before grasping hold of his shaft. I eyed the tip hungrily, wetting my lips before bending down to lick the wetness beading and flowing out of his tip. I felt Max's hands urgently positing my lower half then his tongue licking the entire seam of my sex, from my anus to my clit. It forced a moan out of me, just as my mouth came down over the head of his cock.

He thrust into me then, forcing his cock into my mouth while his tongue speared into my cunt, thrusting into it like a cock, causing me to gasp, allowing Max's cock to go even deeper inside my mouth. I gagged and tried to pull back, but Max's hands had come up to hold me in place.

"Relax Maya," Foster's voice came, right next to my ear. At Foster's urging, I breathed in, forcibly relaxing my muscles and willing calm over myself. I knew that neither of these men would ever try to push me beyond what I could take. I trusted them. Just as I thought that, Max's tight grip on me relaxed and he allowed me up. I took a few deep breaths, then wrapped my hands around the back of Max's thighs and pulled myself back down over his cock. I wanted to take him all the way. I love him, I would do anything for him to give him back the pleasure and the love that he's given me, I thought, as I forced myself to take him more deeply than I ever had before.

I felt him groan inside my pussy as he realized this, then his mouth became a frenzy of movement: open mouthed, wet kisses, thrusting tongue, lips sucking on my clit in abandon. I pulled my face off of his cock and begged, "STOP! Please Max, stop! You're going to make me cum. I can't take it," I panted, trembling with the effort, once again, not to cum. My neck straining downwards, looking underneath me, down the length of my body, trying to find Max's eyes and implore him. All I could see was his chin and his hungry mouth where it was fastened onto my sex, it almost undid me. Then he pulled his mouth away, instinctively knowing I was looking at him, and found my eyes immediately.

"You're so fucking beautiful Maya," Max confessed, planting a chaste kiss at the top of my sex. "I love how much you struggle to please me. You do please me," he admitted vehemently. "More than you will ever know. I love you. I love everything about you." He continued to gaze into my upside down eyes for a few more poignant seconds, before his tongue snaked out and began to tease my clit in slow sensuous flicks, making my eyes shut in pleasure. I groaned, then found his sex again with my mouth, tenderly loving its entire length.

I felt Foster's hands gently ease over the flesh of my ass then, knead the rounded globes. I felt him bend over to kiss each cheek, then I felt his tongue rimming my asshole. The sensation of two mouths on me, one buried in my cunt, the other in my ass was unquestionably one of the most erotic things I'd ever felt. I moaned in pleasure as Max's cock slid into my throat, and his hips gently thrust up and down in tiny increments, fucking my face. I loved everything about that moment.

I pulled myself up to catch my breath and felt Foster's tongue cease in my ass. I could hear his hand sliding up and down his shaft. I could hear his panting breaths. Then I felt the head of his cock sliding through my slick folds, teasing my sex.

Max was sucking on my clit, but I felt his tongue come out to tangle with Foster's cock, where it was teasing my wet folds. The three of us groaning in unison before Foster pulled his cock away, then suddenly thrust it all the way inside of me, in one swift movement, causing my entire body to go rigid. He impaled me to my limits, and a scream ripped from my hoarse throat.

Max's hips were thrusting at the air he was so worked up. I watched his cock bob in front of my eyes and I needed it in my mouth again. Now!

"Fuck her hard," Max growled at Foster, just as my mouth engulfed Max's entire length and I tried to swallow him whole.

Max grunted and thrust into my throat as Foster pulled out and slammed in harder and deeper than before. This time, when I screamed,

Max's cock caught every single vibration along his dick and he turned into a wild animal as the sensations of my vibrating throat made him lose control and begin to fuck my face in earnest. I mastered my fear and panic, and fought hard to tame the urge to choke and gag as I welcomed his roughness.

I welcomed Foster's roughness too. Their wild abandon, my lack of control – it was so freeing and so empowering at the same time. I had no control, and was so completely at both of their mercies, yet I was able to cause them to lose control over themselves, almost to the point that I thought they might hurt me accidentally, – even though I knew, deep down, they never would.

Foster took my pussy hard, driving into my tight cunt with ferocious, primal strokes, pounding at my cervix like he was trying to break through, and grunting like a beast. He bent forward over me to grab my hands and pull my arms behind me, effectively pulling me away from sucking on Max's cock. His beautiful fingers manacled my wrists, as he gripped them to either side of his hips, levering back on them, forcefully, with each potent thrust so he could push himself inside with even more depth and power.

Max resumed sucking on my clit until I thought my eyes might cross from the intensity of the pleasure that I felt welling up inside of my body. I'd never been fucked like this before. Nobody had ever completely let loose inside of me like this and totally owned my body, let alone two somebodies.

I knew there would be no holding back this time. I could feel the force of the orgasm I had held at bay, washing back over my body like a tidal wave. It was inevitable, even more so when I felt Max's tongue slip over my sex where it was joined with Foster's marauding cock. The pleasure of that had me grinding my sex into Max's face and burying my own face back over his cock, sucking it and fucking it with greedy abandon..

Pumping and thrusting and groaning away in complete harmony, the three of us reached some sort of wild nirvana-like plateau of pleasure. We had a fragile and tenuous razor's edge of complete unison that suddenly broke as Foster came inside of me, like a freight train, with one last, giant thrust.

Max bit down almost painfully on my clit and I exploded over his face. My pussy milked every last drop from Foster, as Max let out a howl and began to unload spurt after spurt of hot sticky cum deep in my throat. After a moment, I relaxed my mouth so I could breathe. Cum still pumped out of Max, less forcefully now, filling my mouth and painting my lips as I released his cock.

Max continued to devour my dripping cunt,

licking at Foster's and my combined sexes, where our mingled juices overflowed. He lapped up each spilled drop as if it were ambrosia. My body trembled from the feel of Max's mouth teasing at my over sensitive flesh. Foster wrapped his arms around me and held me there so I could not pull away, forcing me to take the tortuous caress of Max's tongue. He even began to slide in and out of my channel again, causing me even more painful pleasure, while letting loose more of our cum for Max to greedily lap at.

I didn't think it was possible, but I suddenly came again on Foster's slightly softening cock, with Max's lips and tongue masterfully manipulating my cunt. Then I collapsed like a rag doll.

Still lodged deeply inside of my body, Foster lifted me up so he could pile onto the bed and spoon me, one hand grasping for Max to come and wrap us up from the other side.

We lay there, completely sated, in a tangle of sweaty and satisfied limbs. Caressing, kissing, nibbling, fondling, touching, murmuring and sharing until we all drifted off into the deepest, most fulfilling sleeps we'd ever had. We were completely content wrapped up in each other's arms.

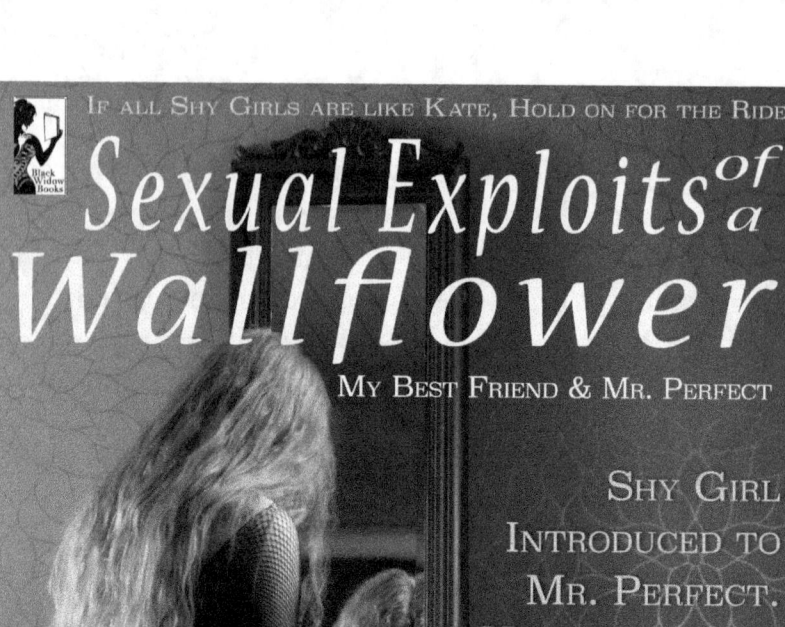

IF ALL SHY GIRLS ARE LIKE KATE, HOLD ON FOR THE RIDE.

Sexual Exploits of a
Wallflower

MY BEST FRIEND & MR. PERFECT

SHY GIRL
INTRODUCED TO
MR. PERFECT.
HE BRINGS HOME
HER BEST FRIEND
FOR A FMF
THREESOME SEX.

Black Widow Books

CASSIDY
PHOENYX

Sexual Exploits of a Wallflower

Cassidy Phoenyx

"You are a very passionate woman and such a great little lover."

"You're always flattering me like that," I pouted playfully, batting my eyelashes.

Our eyes met and he smiled, melting my heart like he always did. His dark brown eyes were dancing with laughter. Man, he was sexy.

We met three years ago at a party. I was instantly drawn to his charismatic charm. I'm kind of a shy, awkward, goofball, and he was my polar opposite. I could hear his laughter the minute I walked through the door. There was a crowd of people around him that were thoroughly interested in everything he had to say. He had a presence about him that just exuded confidence. The funny thing about us shy people is, that confident and outgoing is exactly the type of personality we find ourselves naturally drawn to.

My friend Samantha, introduced us. "Kate, this is Doug, remember I told you about the new vice president of the company that I work for."

I was always a little envious of Samantha's ability to just be part of the crowd. She was a witty, engaging person, that people seemed to flock to. She had gorgeous, long, shiny blonde hair and crystal blue eyes. She was a petite woman with a flat stomach and voluptuous behind. It really was her most evident attribute. Her alabaster skin was smooth and flawless. Her attire was always sexy and feminine, yet never slutty. I must confess, I had a bit of a girl crush on her.

"Oh yes, I remember, Hi Doug," I stammered, offering him my hand. I was sure that I was blushing. Damned social anxiety disorder!

He flashed me a warm smile that went straight to his eyes, and asked me to have a seat while Samantha brought me a cocktail. He was as bright and inviting as a summer's day. "So Kate, tell me about yourself. It seems that you already know a little something about me," he stated, while surveying my face.

He was wearing a snow white button up shirt, with two buttons left undone, just the slightest bit of dark chest hair peeking out. It fit well with his light blue, tight-fitting, Levi jeans. He wore the casual classics, but somehow, he just reeked of money.

I noticed the crinkles around his eyes that came with his sunny smile, and thought about how cute they were. On a woman, they were signs of aging, yet on a man, particularly this one, they added character. His head was shaved bald, which I didn't normally go for, but it worked on him. It was obvious that he worked out. I could see his biceps and flat stomach through the sheerness of his shirt. He was olive skinned, probably Italian, I thought. I hoped he didn't notice me ogling him.

I stared at his lips as he talked. I wondered what they would feel like on my body. Was he a good kisser? He probably was, seeing as he was so at ease with himself. How could he not be?

I began to shift in my seat as I imagined making love to such a masculine, older, powerful man. I guessed that he was probably a skilled, generous, lover that knew how to use his silver tongue and hard throbbing cock skillfully. My tight little cunt heated and moistened at the idea.

I continued fidgeting because the friction brought me gratification. It had been years since I had a proper orgasm. It seemed like the men my age just worried about their own pleasure.

The First Time

They spent about two seconds eating pussy, but expected me to perform head on them to completion. The sex was over within two pumps. It was like they were trying to beat the clock, for Christ sakes. At times, it was so fast that I was left wondering if it had actually happened at all.

He probably had plenty of beautiful, sophisticated women at his beck and call. What would he want with a shy, awkward girl like me? However, he listened to my fumbling attempts at intelligent conversation intently, and looked directly into my eyes as I spoke.

Did I sense a hint of attraction in his deep dark eyes? His pupils seemed to dilate as he glanced at me. It was probably just the alcohol. How could it be anything else?

We got into a conversation about music, books, and food. I earn my living as a chef. I'm very passionate about my food. I can't sleep at night until I create the recipe that is on my mind. I had been trying to write a cookbook of my own for years. Imagine that. I could name it Kate's kitchen. I wasn't really into all those fancy foods. My book would consist of just good old, down-home, American fare, done right.

We sat close together and conversed for hours. We went through plenty of cocktails. The liquid courage loosened up my shy tongue. After a while, it was like there was no one else in the room except us. He made me feel so at ease, typically an alien concept for me. The hours just flew by, and we closed out the party as the morning sun seeped in.

"By the way, Kate, I love your boots," he told me as I was leaving. My boots? That's a weird thing for someone to notice, I thought.

That night, or morning, when I got home, I went straight to my room and brought out my dusty old vibrator. I removed all clothing except for my boots. I put on bright red lipstick, and did my hair up in pigtails. I imagined that Doug was with me. I was one of his colleagues, living out her fantasy, being the dirty little slut from the wrong side of the tracks. I couldn't conceive of being with him any other way.

I placed my cock on the nightstand, and switched on some sultry music to enhance the mood. Laying in bed with my knees bent, I sucked on my finger seductively. I caressed my own body all over until I felt my pussy dampen. Spitting on my finger and jammed it into my crotch, I prepared for penetration.

I tugged at my nipples savagely, swaying my head with the beat of the music. Lifting my hips up off the bed, I shoved a second finger into my asshole. I never did that before. The sensation of a finger in each hole was powerful, it made me horny for a flesh and blood cock.

I used my other hand to tickle my clit, wishing

The First Time

I had more hands. I grabbed my dildo from the nightstand and switched it on. I was hot as hell, and totally ready for it now.

Placing the vibrator into my dripping wet sex, I left one finger in my anus and rubbed my body with my other hand while I pictured Doug on top of me.

"Oh Doug, make me cum," I moaned.

I continued to move with the music, and then raised my hips up and slapped my ass hard. I surprised myself.

"I'm a dirty little whore," I cried. "Beat me into submission."

Plunging the vibrator in and out of my hungry little cunt forcefully, while the finger in my other hole did the same. My pussy wouldn't wait any longer. I came wildly, then collapsed to the bed.

"I have to use this thing more often," I stated out loud to no one in particular. When you live alone it's normal to talk to yourself, isn't it?

After that, I couldn't get him out of my mind and tried to come up with ways to bump into him. (Accidently, of course.) I found out where he lived. I looked him up on Google. Coincidentally, he resided just up the block from me. Isn't that lucky? I drove past his house often like a good little stalker.

When our *chance* meeting finally took place, it was at the local dive bar. A real charming location, complete with a broken down jukebox, and neighborhood winos that evidently never bathed, or had a home for that matter. I frequented there often because no one bothered me there, and I could drink alone peacefully without being propositioned by crazy drunk men. The fellows at the bar only cared about their alcohol. Besides, it was close by.

Luckily, that day, I had taken special care with my appearance. At this type of place, I usually didn't bother.

I was wearing a short soft pink skirt that showed off my well-toned legs, (I am really fond of my legs), and a light pink button up shirt, which displayed my ample bosom proudly. Of course, I had on my tall, black, biker boots, which I wore most of the time. My long, red hair cascaded down my shoulders wildly. I checked my appearance in the mirror by the door. My golden tan from the passing summer was just starting to fade. I believed the extra freckles made me look younger than my twenty-seven years. Not for the first time, I absent-mindedly wished that I were taller. I wore just a hint of mascara to bring out the light in my pale green eyes. I wasn't really into makeup, except for my private role-play, so I had chosen a natural colored gloss that emphasized my pouty lips.

I thought that I heard his boisterous voice while I was in the bathroom, but told myself that

The First Time

I must be imagining things. He had this distinct sound that really should be on the radio. It was so unique. What would Mr. vice president be doing in a place like this?

I was coming back from the bathroom, and I saw he was seated at the bar. He watched me intently as I walked up. He was drinking me in. I flushed and gave him what I hoped was my most dazzling smile.

"What are you doing here?" I asked, as I took the empty seat next to him.

"I could ask you that same question," he smirked. "...and dressed like that." He shook his head.

Oh no. "I didn't think that I would run into anyone," I muttered, embarrassed.

"That's no excuse. You are apparently driving every degenerate in this establishment, crazy."

"They're far too focused on their alcohol."

"You may be right. Well, now you're driving me crazy, like you did that night at the party."

Wow, I drive him crazy? My heart leaped for joy. He placed his hand on my knee. "Really though, Mr. money bags what are you doing here?" I fidgeted.

"Mr. money bags?" he laughed.

Oh, (sigh) he was mocking me. I squirmed in my seat. He began to caress my thigh lightly, watching his hand. I looked down at my leg and placed my hand on top of his. I felt butterflies in my stomach, and my pussy began to moisten hotly. I sucked in my breath, then looked up into his mischievous eyes.

"I've been driving by your house just to see if you were home," he stated sheepishly.

"Really?" My heart skipped a beat. "I have been doing the same thing."

"I am well aware."

He knows… how does he know, I wondered.

"You're wearing those boots again, they are so sexy," he remarked.

Oh wow, is it getting hot in here, I pondered. "No one has ever said that to me before."

"They thought it, they just never had the balls to say it. I don't hold much back."

"I noticed."

"Quit looking at me like that, or I will not be able to control myself. I want to tear those clothes right off of you."

"How am I looking at you?" I questioned coquettishly. He cuts right to the chase, doesn't he?

"Don't be coy with me."

I gulped. I needed a drink. I placed my money on the bar, and motioned for the bartender. I was clearly out of my league.

"What will it be?" The bartender, Bob, wore the mask of a man from the wrong side of the tracks, but his smile brightened up his face. He was a nice guy. He seemed to understand when to keep his distance and when you needed a good chat.

"Hey Bob, I'll just have a rum and diet coke."

He shook his head. "Diet coke, now you're drinking healthy." He laughed at his own joke. He said it every time.

Doug chuckled. His hand was still on my thigh. It was hot.

As soon as I got the drink, I gulped it down thirstily and ordered another. Doug eyed me speculatively. "You drink like that often?"

"When I'm thirsty. It's hot in here."

"It certainly is."

We started to talk about everything, and nothing in particular. It was comfortable. We had a rapport. Two in the morning came quickly. We walked together to my car. He held the door open, and asked me if I was all right to drive. I was. He ran his hand through my hair and gazed into my eyes.

"Kate, you are a beautiful woman. I enjoy spending time with you."

Those butterflies were back. "Thank you," I blurted out. "I had a good time."

He leaned in to kiss me, I met him half-way. We kissed deep, full on the lips. His tongue felt soft and warm as it swirled in my mouth. I could taste the Jack Daniels on his breath. It was intoxicating. My hands were on either side of his face, pulling him deeper into my mouth. His hands were wrapped in my hair. I wanted to fuck him right there in the parking lot. My body was aflame with desire.

I was pretty inexperienced when it came to sex, compared to other women my age. I could count the number of men that I had been with on one hand. Samantha commented on it often, stating that I should get out more and live a little. We had been friends since childhood. She knew everything about me. She was right, of course.

When I wasn't at work cooking up a storm, I was at home doing the same. That was just food though, not men, and definitely not relationships. Doug had definitely been around the block, and not just because he was ten years my senior. He had something that just drew people in. You could tell he was experienced in all things.

Wanting to have sex in public was a new feeling for me. I let my hands explore his bulging biceps. He was so manly. It felt good to be in his arms, like I belonged there.

He ran his hands down my back and pulled me closer, our embrace remained intact. I grabbed his ass. I just had to feel it. It was hard and round like an ass should be, not like the flat one's most men had. He kissed my neck, and waves of desire traveled down my body all the way to my lust-filled pussy. I felt his erection against my thigh.

"We have to get out of here, or I will fuck you right now, in this parking lot. I'm almost to the point where I don't care," he breathed into my ear. His breath was warm against my face. I was reeling. I felt like I was in a daze.

"I don't want to," my voice showed my disappointment.

"It's late, and I have a lot of work to do. Don't worry about it. I will be around."

He gave me one last peck on the lips, and I sat in the driver's seat of my car. He closed the door quietly and I watched him as he walked away.

He turned around to wave at me while getting into his car. "Get some sleep!" he ordered.

Demanding isn't he, I thought. I looked at the clock in my beat up old car and noticed that it was 3:30 A.M. Wow, it's a good thing I don't have work today.

I drove home to my little ranch which I was so proud of. I worked really hard to save up enough money to purchase it on my own. Granted, it was small, and in need of repair, but it was all mine. Well, the bank technically owned it, if you wanted to get into the particulars.

It was a baby blue house with a light pink door and white shutters around the windows. Strange, I know. So was I.

There was shrubbery on either side of the path leading to my white patio. It was the place where I liked to have my morning coffee. I would sit on my porch swing, watching the hummingbirds in the Eastern Redbud tree.

The garden was my proudest thing. I didn't have a clue what I was doing when I planted it, but it worked out. I had fresh tomatoes, honeydew melons, peppers, strawberries, green beans, carrots, and herbs of every kind. It was nice to just be able to pick your food right out of the ground. The tomatoes here are second to none, and they are all mine!

As I walked in my front door, I thought about what Doug had said. He will be around? How? He drives past my house. Will I ever see him again? I hoped so, but I really did have to get some sleep.

I put on my crappy old sweats, pulled my hair into a ponytail and climbed right into bed. My sleep was filled with dreams of Doug and our passionate exchange. "I will fuck you right here in this parking lot," was running through my mind. I wished that he had.

I woke with a start and jumped out of bed staring at the clock. Noon, I had slept the whole day away. I padded over to the coffee maker, turned it on, and checked my cell phone. Five missed messages, my mom, my sister, my work, and a number that I was not familiar with. I wondered who it could be, and listened to the messages. Mom wanted me to call her back, work wanted to know if I could fill in tonight, my sister Jen wanted to hang out, and Doug wanted to know if I had made it home alright. He called!

He left two messages. He seemed worried. How did he get my number? I had to gather up the courage to call him back. I distracted myself by making my coffee. I like my coffee strong and tan. It had to be just the right color or it was garbage. Oh to just be normal and call someone without worrying about every little thing you said, what was that like?

I sat down with my coffee, took a deep breath, and returned his call.

"Doug speaking," he answered all business like.

"H-hello," I spoke softly.

"Is this Kate?" he sounded happy to hear from me, delighted even.

"Yea, it's me."

"I was worried about you, why didn't you call me back sooner?"

"I just woke up," I answered, embarrassment filling my voice. "How did you get my number?"

"Oh, I have my ways, rest assured."

What? "Umm okay."

"How did you sleep?" He sounded amused.

"Pretty good considering I just woke up."

"I never sleep. I thought of you all day. I want to ravish you."

Wow, I didn't see that coming. "I had a great time last night," I stuttered. I thought of his mouth on mine.

"Yea me too. What are you doing next Friday?"

"I don't know," I gulped. He wants to see me again!

"Don't make any plans, I'll meet up with you. We'll figure something out. I have to get back to work."

He hung up without saying goodbye. That's kind of rude, I thought.

I went about my day in the usual fashion; Sitting on my porch swing, sipping my coffee, watching the hummingbirds, but my mind kept turning back to Doug. Wow, he was something else, and so arrogant. He had every right to be, of course. He was extremely intelligent and hard working. People seemed to gravitate towards him, myself included. He had a master's degree in psychology, yet chose against it as a career. Deciding instead to work his way up the ranks in the field of advertising. It was no great mystery why he was so good at public speaking. He had been marketing himself for years.

I climbed into the shower and the hot water massaged my skin, while thoughts of Doug raced through my mind. I thought of his masculine hands caressing my body, and his tongue invading my mouth.

My mind wandered and so did my hands. I tweaked my nipples until they stood erect, and my hands traveled slowly downwards towards my most sensitive spot, all the while imagining that my hands were actually his.

I pictured him there and it felt so real. I smoothed over my firm belly. I tugged at my thighs and grabbed my own ass. I was purposely avoiding the spot that I knew would bring me relief in order to tease myself.

When I finally couldn't take anymore, I softly tickled my clitoris. It was aching for gratification. I pretended I was kissing him like we did in the parking lot, only this time, naked. I could almost feel his tongue in my mouth and his hard body rubbing up against mine. I had a wild imagination. I was panting as I threw myself back against the shower wall. He shoved me there, in my mind, and it felt so good.

I plunged two fingers deep into my vagina, holding them there for a minute, still tickling my clitoris with my other hand. I brought my fingers back out, but not all the way, resting them just at the opening. Then I shoved three fingers further into me. I like it rough sometimes. I rapidly pumped my fingers in and out as quickly as I could, groaning in the throes of rapture until I climaxed. My legs were shaking. I had to lie on the shower floor for a moment. It was so intense. The water brought me back to reality, and I continued to lather up as if nothing happened. I needed that release.

I was glad to fill in at work for Dana that night, so I could stop all my silly daydreaming. There is nothing like sweaty hours slaving in the kitchen to get your mind off your troubles, or pleasures. I spent the week in constant anticipation. How will he meet up with me? He hadn't called. I was beginning to lose all hope when he finally touched base. Isn't that just the way things always work out?

I was lying on my couch, in my usual hideous sleepwear, flicking through channels, when I heard a knock on my door. Who could that be? I am not a fan of the pop in. Family members would sneak up on me often to frighten me. They thought it was funny. I didn't. I startle easily, especially at night.

I tried to see who it was by peeking out through the window, but saw no one there. I slowly made my way to the door. I opened the door, and Doug burst through it. I screamed my foolish head off. He laughed uncontrollably, throwing his head back in glee.

"What the heck is wrong with you?" I questioned with my hands on my hips.

He put his hands up as if to say 'awe shucks' or truce. "I'm sorry, I told you that we would get together."

"You never said that you would just show up, in the middle of the night, unannounced." I sounded a little harsh, but I was kind of perturbed with him.

He pulled me in close and kissed me, I didn't resist. All was forgiven.

He smelled delicious and looked that way too. He was wearing a sharp, midnight blue, impeccably fitted, suit and tie that probably cost a fortune. He had on a pale blue, button up, shirt. I love a man in a suit. Even unattractive men look good in suits.

I was suddenly aware of my disgusting attire. "I look a mess, where have you been?"

"I couldn't get you out of my mind," he breathed into my ear, his voice throaty and laced with desire. "Those eyes." He gazed directly into mine. His eyes burned with intensity. "Those lips." He trailed his finger across my lips. "That hair." He ran his hands through my hair. "I couldn't sleep. My mind was filled with thoughts of you."

He breathed. "I was on your doorstep last night," he paused, "I wanted to knock on your door and take you in my arms, but I wasn't sure. I didn't know how you felt."

It seemed like a dream. I didn't know what to say. What if he was full of crap and I exposed too much of my soul to him? I didn't want to scare him off. I had my share of men smooth talking me and heading for the hills when I opened up.

I breathed in the scent of him. My pulse quickened. I wanted him so badly. I didn't know how to proceed from here. I struggled to find the words. Then he kissed me deeply, full on the lips. I could feel his yearning. My body was burning with mutual desire. There was a chemistry that could not be denied. My hands explored his body. I had goose bumps.

"Why didn't you knock?" I caught my breath, Before I could stop them, the words were out of my mouth. "I feel the same." I could feel his cock against my thigh, begging for attention. I felt weak in the knees. No one else has ever affected me like this. I didn't know how to behave.

Inside my mind, hidden away from public view, lived a desirable, sex kitten, yearning to be free. I had drawers full of sexy attire that I never had the courage to wear. I had naughty thoughts I never had the balls to share. I would act them out in my mind, by myself, without prejudice. I was uncomfortable with my own sexuality. I was afraid of people, but he changed all that...

"I'm a busy man, Kate. You could never look a mess."

"Smooth," I grinned up at him.

"I could be smooth," he teased.

"I wouldn't doubt it for a moment."

Oh, this man. I had only spent two days with him, but they were so packed with heartfelt conversations, that I felt like I had known him for a long time. I liked him and I hoped that he liked me. I led him to my couch, then offered him a drink. Handing him the flicker, I headed towards the kitchen to pour two glasses of red wine. I scoured the cabinets for some type of snack. My father taught me to always serve refreshments to a houseguest. I decided on cheese and crackers, always a crowd pleaser.

I placed the refreshments on the coffee table, and took a seat next to him on the sofa. Handing him his wine, I said cheers, and we clinked glasses.

After taking a sip, we placed our wine on the table and he attacked me. He wrapped me in his arms, and devoured me with his sweet kisses. He sure was eager, I thought.

I allowed my hands to wander over his body freely. It was good to finally be alone with him. I removed his suit jacket, caresseing his shoulders. He loosened his tie, and started to unbutton his shirt. I pushed his hands away. I wanted to unwrap this present.

I looked into his eyes, slowly removed his tie and unbuttoned his shirt. It was incredibly erotic. I got a good look at his brawny chest and shoulders while I let his shirt drop to the floor. He had the tiniest bit of dark chest hair. It was unusual to see that on men anymore. I liked it. It gave him an edge and reminded me of our age difference. Maybe I could pretend to be his naughty student and he could be the disciplinarian, I pondered. I caressed him sensuously and planted soft kisses all over his chest.

"You are so sexy, Kate."

My name sounded like music coming from his lips, like a symphony composed just for me. At that moment, there was no doubt in my mind, that he really meant what he had said. He looked at me so earnestly.

"So are you," I breathed.

I pulled him up to a standing position and fumbled with his belt. I couldn't quite work it, so he took over while I admired the view. Wow, he was a magnificent creature. He was muscular but not overly so. When he removed his belt, I took it from there. I unbuttoned and unzipped his pants, letting them gently slide down his legs, feeling the heat coming from his body and savored every moment of it.

The First Time

I noticed he wore 'tighty-whities', I removed them. I caught my first glimpse of his thoroughly erect and rather large package, as I grabbed ahold of his cock and massaged it carnally.

Dropping to my knees, as if to worship at his altar of paradise, I flashed him my most alluring smile, and took his member into my mouth greedily. I could feel his eyes upon me, so I gazed up at him and we shared a silent, heated exchange of power. He grabbed at the back of my hair, tugged at it, and wrapped it around his hands. He shoved my head all the way down on his juicy cock. It went pretty deep into the back of my throat and I had to concentrate on not gagging. My eyes watered from the immense pressure. I slowly manipulated my head back and forth, getting his penis as far into my mouth as I could, and then letting up so that I was just grazing the tip with my lips. My tongue licked the tip tenderly. He persisted to push and pull on my head with his hands wound in my hair. He slowly increased the speed and force. I massaged his balls gently, and continued worshiping his magnificent manhood. I gasped for air after his massive bulge stuffed me to the gills.

"Oh I'm going to cum," he grunted.

I didn't mind and I moved my head more vigorously so that I could help him along. He was breathing heavily, and I felt like some kind of hot pornstar, desired by all.

"Oh –oh –oh," he groaned.

Suddenly my mouth was filled with his jizz and thick, hot, salty liquid spilled out the sides. I released my mouth and swallowed what remained of his semen. Delicious!

I grabbed his cock once again and guided the rest of his ejaculation out with my delicate hands. That was fun. I felt like a dirty little whore, and I loved every moment of it.

He carefully pulled my sweatshirt up over my head. I had no undergarments on. I never wore them, not if I could help it. He kissed my shoulders and licked my nipples seductively. I stood up, tugging at my sweatpants to be free of them. My pussy was burning hot and soaking wet from watching what I could do to a grown man. I really wanted him to take me right now. His rough hands explored my body and tantalized my smooth skin.

"You are so hot," he breathed throatily.

He rubbed my thighs roughly, sending shockwaves of pleasure spiraling throughout my body. I rocked my hips towards his hands to give him a clue. I needed release. My loins were crying out to me. Oh, the sweet torment. Finally, his finger found its way to my lust filled sex.

"Aaah-oooh,'" I let out an unintelligible guttural sound.

"Baby, you're so wet," he declared.

He dropped to his knees and licked my clitoris tenderly while exploring my crevice with two fingers. He plunged deeper into me, I cried out again. He thrust his fingers in and out, harder and harder, then added two more fingers to the assault.

I watched him as he pleasured me. It was sexy as hell. I had never watched before. He was so into what he was doing. I grasped his back and shoulders roughly. I needed something to hold onto.

The heat coming from his body felt like a furnace working overtime in the dead of winter. He removed his fingers from my pussy, and his luscious tongue took their place. I wasn't ready for that. Wow, did it feel heavenly. His tongue swirled around, deep within my crotch, and his finger rapidly encircled my clitoris.

He grabbed my behind with his other hand and pulled me closer to him, forcing his tongue deeper into my steamy sex. It seemed like he was touching the back of my vagina from the inside. I cried out in delight. His tongue twisted around like a whirlpool. I struggled to stand. I felt weak in the knees and my heart was beating rapidly. I squeezed my hands harder around his shoulders to gain more leverage. He smacked my ass then rubbed it. I squealed. He stroked my ass harder and I moaned loudly. He slapped my rump again, and again, while his tongue retained its position in my pussy.

"Oh spank me harder, oh that feels so good."

I could not believe that I just said that! A shy innocent girl like me, speaking dirty like that? It did feel good, though. It was a sensation that I had never experienced before. Each time that he hit me, his tongue plunged further into my core. The sting lasting for a second, then my ass burned in a good way. After each spank, he rubbed my bottom. I felt my insides begin to quiver, and I leaned my head back and moaned noisily. My climax erupted like a volcano, leaving me shaking from the aftershocks, and draining the energy out of me.

I grabbed Doug's hand and led him over to the couch, where I rested my head on his lap for a moment to gain my composure. He ran his fingers through my sweaty, mangled hair, and we cuddled for a while. He lifted my head up by the chin to meet his and stared directly into my eyes.

"Where have you been all my life?" He questioned, his eyes brimming with passion.

I beamed at him and threw my arms around his neck. I showered him with kisses. It was pretty emotional. He chuckled softly. We embraced each other for a while, and things began to heat up once more.

Our hands explored one another's bodies

unabashedly. We were lying side by side. I grabbed his toned ass and thrust my hips into him. I felt his warm, sticky cock jump at attention from the unexpected friction. I wanted him inside of me.

He covered my mouth with his, and our tongues mingled together. I felt my body respond to the closeness. He leaned into me and guided me flat onto the couch with his weight so that I was lying on my back, and he was on top. He placed his hands on either side of me. The kiss was deep and intense, and it left me breathless. Our bodies were on fire.

The skin on skin sensation drove me wild. We were slick with perspiration. Doug slithered up and down while still connected to my mouth. I clawed at his firm, strong back. He took one of his hands and reached between my legs, exploring my wetness tenderly.

I sighed loudly, and reached down in between us searching for his rock hard cock. I took it into my hand and stroked up and down. It was like a burning ember.

I felt pre-cum trickle out of the head when I placed my thumb gently over the tip. The sensation of the temperature difference made him moan with euphoria. We seemed to reach the conclusion that we could no longer bear this sweet torture at the same time. His hand came out from between my legs, and mine wrapped around his shoulders simultaneously. His spectacular shaft slowly entered my crotch, inch by agonizing inch. I grasped his shoulders tighter and rammed him into me. I cried out his name in ecstasy.

"Doug, Oh Doug, oh my god!"

He gazed at me and picked up speed, thrusting in and out of my pulsating pussy. I wrapped my legs around his back tightly, squeezing the life out of him. He felt remarkable inside of me.

I matched his moves. We were both breathing and panting heavily. I reached my hands between our legs and cupped his balls softly. I placed my fingers in a ring around the back of his shaft and squeezed, sliding my hand back and forth as much as I could. I felt my own labia slamming against my fingers. It was so freaking hot. I fucking lost it!

"Holy shit, I'm going to cum," he screamed.

"Oh no, not yet," I pleaded.

I was so close. My slit was tightening and loosening on his jumbo-sized penis.

"Sorry darling," he couldn't control it any longer.

He pulled out just in time, releasing the flood gates all over my belly. At that exact moment, my pussy tensed up and spurted a messy orgasm that leaked down the sides of my vagina and onto my couch. That was a first. We climaxed together like you read about in books. It actually happened. It did. He rubbed his cum into my stomach.

The First Time

We were soaked in love juice and sweat. My hair was sex mangled and knotted up.

"I don't know about you but I could really use a shower," I proclaimed, and gulped down what was left of my wine.

"Yup, shower time. Let's go."

I grabbed us two towels from the closet and led the way, smacking him playfully on the behind. We lathered each other up, and took a long, hot, luxurious shower.

"Your ass is nice and pink. It looks so hot," he exclaimed salaciously.

"Well, I've been a bad girl. I deserved a good hiding," I replied coquettishly. My face flushed with embarrassment. I hoped he didn't notice.

"That you did and I am just the man for the job." He snickered.

"Oh, you are just the man for any job."

We played and chatted the whole time. I could actually fall for Doug, I warned myself. I needed to tread lightly and protect my heart. After his departure, I fell asleep as soon as my head hit the pillow. I dreamt that we lived together, and I could have him by my side, and inside of me, forever.

In the weeks that followed, we became quite the item. His boisterous personality, and my reserved ways, complimented each other beautifully. He brought me out of my shell a little, and sometimes I taught him to hold his tongue. He could be a bit blunt and biting with his words.

We always had a good time, and never ran out of things to say to each other. He treated me to many things that I had never before experienced, and I am not just talking sexually. He took me places that I could never afford and treated me like a queen.

I cooked for him often. It was nice to have someone around to taste my recipes. He encouraged me to continue on my path of completing my cookbook. He enjoyed food as much as I did, and understood the work, love, and passion that went into preparing a meal properly.

I told him about the men before him, and how I had never really enjoyed sex all that much. He told me that I had just never met the right one. He said that I was a passionate woman, who had many unexplored talents. He didn't understand why I lacked the confidence to pursue my dreams to their fullest.

We spoke of our fantasies. He didn't have many that weren't realized, but I did. I was still too intimidated to share all of my desires with him, so I continued with my private role-playing. I went out to lunch with Samantha and could not stop staring at her delicious ass.

" What are you looking at?" she asked.

"Nothing," I stated, feeling the heat flood my cheeks.

"You're staring at my ass."

The First Time

" N-no I-I..." My voice drifted off as I searched for the words.

"Hey, it's okay. I'm used to it. Besides, I sneak peeks at your breasts every once in a while. It doesn't make you gay, you know."

"No, I know. I just..." I was stunned. She looks at my breasts? When?

"You don't have to act so shocked, you're a beautiful woman," she joked, shoving a forkful of pasta into her mouth.

"I-I'm not!" I declared trying to muster up the strength to get through this awkward conversation with my dignity intact.

"Oh Kate," she giggled, rolling her eyes at me. "Look I'm just saying, if you fantasize about me, that's cool with me."

"Um... okay." What more could I say?

"Now, tell me all about Daddy Warbucks. I feel like I haven't seen you in ages."

Oh good, she wants to talk about Doug. I could handle that, I thought. "You do work with him."

"For him," she pouted. "I mean, what is he like?"

"Well, he's sweet and sexy...."

"Yeah I know he's sexy, I've seen him. I have eyes. I meant, what is he like in bed. I've been dreaming of him for months and you go and land him. I introduced you, I'm so jealous." She put her face in her hands in a gesture of mock exasperation.

I giggled. She's so silly. "He's out of this world in bed. He's fucking amazing. He's so experienced." My voice drifted off.

We giggled together like schoolgirls. Oh, schoolgirls... That gave me a naughty idea.

"Well, he is quite a bit older than us, and you hardly have any experience at all."

Oh no, not this again, I thought. She's always mentioning my lack of sexual exploration.

"You have to be careful with a man like that, Kate."

"What does that mean?"

"He's used to getting everything he wants, when he wants it, you know?"

I did know. It worried me. Maybe I wasn't good enough for him. I doubted myself. There was just no way that I was going to stay away from him, though.

After lunch, I went home to my empty house, and thought about what Samantha had said. She would be cool with it if I fantasized about her. Did she fantasize about me, I wondered. I went into my bedroom to think more clearly.

I opened up my dresser drawer, and selected my short, pink checkered, schoolgirl skirt. I chose a tight-fitting, white, button-up shirt, and black chunky heeled Mary Jane shoes. I dressed in them deliberately. I styled my hair into a braid that hung down the back of my neck down to my ass. I checked my image in the mirror. I undid three buttons of my shirt, and allowed my breasts to nearly pop out. I thought about Samantha peeking at my bosom.

Wow, I looked like a dirty little schoolgirl. It was just the image that I was going for. I added dark blush to my cheeks, and plenty of black makeup around my eyes. I switched on my iPod and danced around the room. I felt myself up as I swayed from side to side. I pictured myself being spied on in my sexy attire. That was a hot idea. Maybe I should share my sick fantasies with Doug. How would I bring it up?

I caressed my large breasts with vigor. I kneaded my thighs gently, and squealed with delight at the sensations it caused. I sauntered over to the nightstand, and grabbed my battery-operated cock. I shouldn't leave this thing lying about, what if Doug sees it? Then my twisted little mind imagined the things that he could do with it.

My fingers slid up my skirt and tickled my clit. My freshly shaved pussy was damp and ready for sex. I laid down on the bed, spreading my legs wide open. I leaned up slightly so that I could see my spread-eagled slit in the full-length mirror across the room. It was so fucking sexy. I turned the vibrator on, and brought it towards my crotch slowly. I wanted to watch my pussy open as it entered me. I fondled my clitoris and watched it engorge.

Samantha was right there with me in my mind. I pretended it was her fingers caressing me. My vagina widened and welcomed the toy into its folds. I left it there for a moment, admiring the view. I opened up like a flower in bloom. I could feel the desire burning in my belly. I remembered how glorious it felt when I had a finger in my anus, so I shoved one up there.

"Oh god!" I cried out. I plunged the vibrator further into my slick sex. I manipulated my hand-held cock in and out of me, to the rhythm of the music. I was the conductor of my body's own symphony. My wetness dripped down and lubricated my asshole. I decided to try two fingers to see if I could handle it. It felt so freaking awesome! I climaxed almost immediately. I violently shook and screamed out Samantha's name in the throes of rapture.

I sank back to the bed and let my nameless penis fall to the floor. As my heartbeat came back to normal and my vision cleared, I noticed that my once closed bedroom door was slightly ajar. I sat bolt upright as fear crept into my body.

Doug walked through the door like nothing out of the ordinary had taken place. "What are you doing?" He inquired with a knowing look.

I was mortified. "Um, I don't uh…"

He looked downright amused. "Look, you don't have to be embarrassed. Everyone plays with themselves." He glanced at the discarded vibrator, then back at me. "I would have thought it was my name you would call out."

"It is, usually." I stared down at the floor, ashamed.

He picked up the sex toy and placed it on the nightstand. "Oh, the things we will do with this." His voice was dripping with desire.

He took a seat next to me on the bed. I mustered up the strength to bring my gaze off the floor. I noticed that his cock was straining against the fabric of his pants, which looked uncomfortably tight.

"How long were you watching me?" My voice was small.

"Long enough to cause this." He followed my gaze to his saluting package. I was openly fixated on his immense bulge. It was hard to look away, like staring directly into an eclipse. "I didn't want to interrupt, but I was about to take matters into my own hands."

"You scared the crap out of me! You shouldn't just walk into people's houses," I scolded, peeling my eyes away from his sensational shaft.

"You were so unbearably hot. I felt naughty watching you, it added to my enjoyment."

"Was I?"

"I didn't know that you were into chicks. How come you never told me?"

"I don't tell you everything." I tried to sound mysterious. I was thinking about my imaginary role-playing.

"Do you think of her while we are making love?"

"Who?" I gulped.

"You know full well. Do you?"

"No, never with you. I don't think of anything else but us."

"Did you two ever hook up? Do you still?" He sounded turned on, with just a hint of jealousy peeking through his voice.

"No, Doug it's not like that. I just find her attractive." My voice was weak, and I stared at my hands.

"Well she is extremely attractive, I can't blame you for that. Would you ever act on it?"

Oh, god, this was humiliating. I thought about Samantha peering at my chest and turned crimson red. "She caught me peeking at her ass," I confessed, sounding small.

He laughed wholeheartedly. "Who hasn't ogled her ass? That girl has a better booty than a Kardashian."

"She told me that she peeks at my breasts, and she doesn't mind if I fantasize about her."

The First Time

He shifted, adjusting his cock in his pants. Our conversation was making him hornier. "Well, maybe we could share her. It would be a conflict of interest seeing as how she works with me," he cleared his throat, "Under me... um, for me... I'm her boss is what I mean. Oh god, that sounds dangerous and sexy as fuck." His voice was raspy and laced with desire.

"This is turning you on?" I asked incredulously.

"Hey, I'm only trying to help you out," he fibbed, with a devious grin on his face.

"Oh, knock it off, you heathen." I playfully shoved his arm.

"Hey, I am the one who came here to find my girlfriend fantasizing about someone else, and treating her body like an amusement park." He held his hand to his chest in mock pain.

I giggled. He was so cute.

"You mind helping a fellow out." He motioned towards his manhood.

I jumped up into his lap and wrapped my legs around his back. His jeans felt rough against my sensitive cunt. I wrapped my arms around his neck. We were face to face. He tugged on my braid.

"By the way, I love the get-up." His eyes traveled up and down my outfit appraisingly. "Really sexy."

I planted a big wet kiss on his mouth. He rubbed my back with his strong hands. I ground my pussy into his cock, and kissed his neck. He lifted me off his lap placing me on the ground in a standing position, then he stood up as well.

"Hang on a minute, we can't get anything done like this." He undid his pants and threw them on the floor. He sat back down on the bed, and motioned for me to come hither. "You may proceed."

He left his shirt, and socks on. He looked silly. I smiled to myself and sat back in his lap, assuming our original position. Our bare sex organs were touching each other. I began to grind in his lap. He kissed me. His skilled tongue spiraled around in my mouth. His manhood seemed to stiffen further by the second. He placed his hand between my legs, and felt my crotch. He slid a finger in with ease.

"You're always so ready for me," he remarked. He grabbed one of my hands and positioned it upon my sex.

"Feel how wet you are." I stuck a finger inside of myself. We each had a finger in my sex. His cock was smashed up against my hand. I used my thumb to tease his package. I was aflame with desire.

I lifted my ass up a little, maneuvering myself so that I could wiggle my clit against his bulge. I gazed seductively into his eyes and jiggled on top of him.

I removed my finger from where it

was, grabbed his hands and placed them on my breasts. He massaged them obligingly. I positioned his shaft at my slit. I felt the sensation of him filling me up as he eased himself in. I sat down, and my pussy was stuffed with cock. It was so deep. I rocked in his lap, our bodies grinding together. I contracted my internal muscles on his member. We were panting like thirsty animals. He enveloped me in his arms and kissed me wildly.

"Oh baby, you are so hot," he breathed through gritted teeth.

"Holy shit!" I shouted as my pussy squirted hot liquid all over his cock.

"I want to cum inside you, aaah..." he breathed lifting me off his lap, and standing me on the floor.

I kneeled before him, grabbed his package and stroked it. I placed my mouth on his member, and lapped up the jizz that oozed down my throat. It was warm, thick, and salty.

He had turned me into a wanton sex goddess. He cupped the back of my head tenderly and sighed. I looked up at him. Damn, he was gorgeous. There is something so spectacular about kneeling before your man.

In the weeks that followed, we discussed inviting Samantha into our bedroom often. The contemplation made us hot, and we role-played scenes that lived in our dirty minds. Many thoughts raced through my head. How could I make it happen? Did I really want to do this? What if he liked her better than me? Would he think she was prettier than me? What would happen if she were a better fuck than me? She's obviously more experienced. I mean, a fantasy is one thing, but the actual event may, or may not live up to the dream. We would have to wait and see.

I invited Samantha over for dinner. I had plenty of red wine on hand to perform my seduction. I prepared prosciutto and cheese stuffed lamb tenderloin, roasted rosemary potatoes and green beans almandine. I served oysters on the half shell, and bruschetta as an appetizer. I was pulling out all the stops. I had the lights down low, and soft mood music playing in the background. Underneath the chandelier, in the middle of my dining room table, stood a large crystalline vase full of bright, rich, purple orchids and violet anthuriums. Pearl plates and gleaming silverware sat atop of a crimson, red velvet tablecloth. I poured the chilled wine in crystal glasses, set the bottle back into the ice bucket, then went to get dressed for the evening.

I chose a slinky, little, dark red, dress that clung to every curve of my body, and exhibited a significant amount of cleavage. I put on strappy, sparkly, dark red, sandals. I checked my image in the mirror. I looked hot! If I do say so myself. I allowed my long, red hair to spiral down my shoulders untamed. I ran dark mascara over my lashes, and spread bright red lipstick across my pouty lips. Who could resist such a tantalizing sight? There was a knock at the door...

The delicious smells coming from the kitchen greeted Samantha upon her arrival.

"Oh wow Kate, you really went all out."

"We aim to please," I quipped, allowing my words to hang in the air.

She handed me a bottle of wine, and I led her to the dining room.

"You look fabulous! Is this a date?" She inquired half jokingly.

I felt the blood rush to my cheeks. "Do you want it to be?" I propositioned courageously.

"You really look hot." She stated, ignoring my question.

"Thank you. So do you," I almost whispered, sheepishly.

I allowed myself to check her out. Her shiny blonde hair piled atop of her head loosely, in a messy bun with tendrils hanging, framing her beautiful face. She wore a soft pink, lacy, see-through top that accentuated her figure. Her black leather mini-skirt was filled to the limit by her robust bottom. Her crystal blue eyes shone with excitement. I could hardly wait to get my hands on her.

I pulled out a chair at the dining room table and motioned for her to have a seat. I brought a crystal platter full of food to the table, and sat down beside her. We picked up our glasses of wine, clinked them together, and said, "cheers."

"What a delicious looking spread, I hardly know where to start."

I suddenly realized how hungry I was. We devoured our dinner savagely. It was mouth-wateringly good.

"I've said this before, you can actually cook your ass off."

"Why, thank you." I smiled at her whole-heartedly.

When I stood up to reach for an oyster, I accidently (on purpose) brushed against her side. Electricity sparked through my body, and I was sure that she felt the same. Flames of desire illuminated her face as she smiled up at me. The atmosphere in the room heated, as the temperature between us shot up. Our eyes locked. She slowly pulled out her chair, and rose to her feet.

We pounced on one another ferociously, like bloodthirsty animals. I could hardly contain myself. I was a steaming pot about to boil over. Our hands traveled all over one another's bodies. She grabbed a fistful of my hair, and planted a full, juicy kiss on my lips.

Thunder crashed outside. We turned our heads to follow the sound. The front door sprung open, lightening radiated on Doug's face as he waltzed in the door. I had timed my devious plan perfectly.

He did not speak a word. He just sauntered up to us. He collected fistfuls of both our hair, then pushed our lips together. We obliged and our tongues sparred in each other's mouths passionately. It was hypnotic, like we were all under some sort of sex spell.

"You girls are so fucking hot. I am a lucky man!" he grunted.

I could not believe this was happening. Doug caressed our bodies as we continued our ardent tongue tango.

"Oh god, what am I going to do with you ladies?" His voice was raspy.

Apparently, he decided to take the lead in this torrid encounter. He took us each by the hand and led us to the bedroom. We followed along silently. After all, he was the boss.

We sat down on the bed staring up at him. He stood over us. We waited for instruction like obedient little schoolgirls.

I had no clue what to do next. He looked like he was deep in thought. He caressed our cheeks tenderly. An unscrupulous smile slowly spread across his face. He stuck a thumb in each of our mouths. We sucked feverishly. He pulled us up off the bed by the hand.

"Take off your clothes," he ordered.

We obeyed. He pulled me to him and kissed me. He removed his tie. He used it to fasten my wrist to a bedpost. He used one of my silk scarves to blindfold me. Oh man, I didn't know what I was in for. My legs were bound together by some kind of rope. I was not sure exactly.

I gasped, not knowing what was about to occur. It was too late. I had given up complete control. Hands were touching me everywhere. My senses were heightened. There was a hand on each of my breasts, rough hands. They must be Doug's. There were feminine hands caressing my thighs. I tried to move but could not. The feeling was intense. I cried out in ecstasy. My pussy was on fire from this agonizing assault. I needed something inside of me now.

"Please," I begged. The hands started traveling all over my body again. I lost track of which hand was whose. They were teasing me everywhere except for the one place that would bring me relief. Then two hands left me. I heard the door open and footsteps walking away. The hands that remained were soft and petite. They belonged to Samantha.

"What are you doing to me?" I demanded.

"Relax," she commanded. "Doesn't it feel good?"

Yes, it did, I thought. All I could do was nod.

I felt Doug's presence reenter the room. There

was a wet, cold sensation on one of my nipples. Water trickled down my breast. An ice cube, I thought. Another ice cube traveled down my stomach. It was cool and wet, yet so very hot at the same time. Water filled up my belly button. My crotch needed mercy. I had never felt anything like this before. A velvety soft tongue flicked my nipples one at a time.

"Holy Christ!" I yelled.

Next the tongue was on my neck, then it was around my earlobes. Warm breath breathed into my ears sending waves of desire all the way through my body, and down to my extremely wet and dripping hot sex. A finger plunged into my folds. I almost came immediately. It felt fan-fucking-tastic.

I lifted and lowered my hips like a wanton whore. I had no idea who belonged to that finger, but I did not care. Then it was gone.

"No!" I cried and sat up slightly, my restraints hampering free movement.

The finger was replaced with a delicate tongue. Silky hair teased my thighs. I threw my head back and whimpered aloud. I was pushed back down on the bed. Doug straddled my chest and rubbed the tip of his throbbing cock against my lips. I opened my mouth and sucked on it hungrily. He rocked his hips back and forth, bringing his penis deeper into my mouth with each push. His package tickled the back of my throat. I almost gagged.

Samantha continued to lap at my lust-filled slit. I lost my damned mind! My orgasm came violently while my mouth was still stuffed with cock. Semen squirted down my throat. I felt like I was going to choke. I tried to scream, but I could not. Fluids spilled out of me, and I was rocked to my core. The bed underneath my ass was soaking wet.

Doug slid off of me as I gasped for air. Samantha stopped her assault. Doug took the blindfold off my face and freed me from my restraints. I had to adjust my eyes to the lights in the room. I sat up. Thunder continued to crash outside.

"You are so damn hot." He kissed me.

My throat felt raw. My pussy was engorged and sensitive to each movement of my body. It was wonderful.

We were all thirsty, and I needed a break, so we went back into the dining room and polished off both bottles of wine. We sat at the table naked and talked like old friends. Doug ate some of the food that Samantha and I had not finished. He was a hungry man.

The wine began to make us all feel amorous once more. We made our way back into the bedroom. I gave Samantha a big wet kiss, and pulled her down onto the bed. Doug grabbed the vibrator off my nightstand. Samantha and I lay facing each other kissing. Doug positioned himself between my legs, and teased my clit with the tip of his penis. He turned the vibrator on and rubbed it against Samantha's clitoris. His cock was coming back to life.

He grabbed Samantha's ass as he plunged his member deep inside me. I could feel his bulge continue to engorge within my core. He moved his hand over Samantha's sex to make sure she was ready.

He worked the toy in and out of her while his package remained planted deep within me. He moaned, and growled out loud. Samantha squirmed around whimpering and thrusting her hips. We were on our backs now, with our sides, arms, and legs touching. I rocked my hips from side to side. Thunder crashed outside. Samantha cried out. I could tell she was nearing the end.

I moved my hand to her golden pussy to help her along. I rubbed her clit firmly as Doug continued to plunder her cunt with the dildo.

Sweat was beading on Samantha's beautiful body, her cries became louder and more rhythmic. I knew she was about to orgasm. I watched as it happened. I saw her sex erupt as sticky fluid leaked down the sides of her thighs spilling all over my bed. It was damn sexy.

Once her aftershocks had subsided, she climbed

up and sat on my face. I lapped up her sticky juices, and plunged my tongue into her vagina. I spiraled it around inside her. She jumped at times because her crotch was still overly sensitive from her climax.

Doug pounded his throbbing member in and out of me rapidly and vigorously. He smacked Samantha on her butt, then stuck a finger in her anus. We must have been a sight, mangled together like that. My climax came without warning. The clamping of my vaginal muscles sent Doug over the edge. He pulled out of me, stroking his cock to ejaculation, spurting all over Samantha's ample bottom. It dripped from her ass to my chest. I felt her muscles tighten on my tongue, and her juices flowed down my throat. She let out a primal cry as she ground herself into my face. We collapsed in a heap on the bed panting and sweating.

We were a cum covered, sticky, mess, so we decided to take a shower. We helped each other lather up, and washed one another's hair. We spoke about our adventure and made a pact to never tell anyone. We remained under the steamy water until it finally ran cold. We changed my messy sheets, then all slid back into my bed together and watched some television. We fell asleep in each other's arms.

We woke up to the sound of birds chirping. I put on my clothes as Samantha raided my closet.

The First Time

She was looking for something she could wear to work, which would fit her ass. Doug was putting on the clothes he had worn last night.

As they got dressed, I made my way to the kitchen and turned on the coffee pot. I fried up some bacon and eggs. We sat down together and had a lively conversation over breakfast. There was no awkwardness. It all felt natural. Together we cleared up the dishes and left them soaking for later.

We had to leave for work. Dressed and ready to go, we left the house together. The storm clouds were giving way to a beautiful sunrise. There in the east was a newly formed Rainbow. Samantha and I caught sight of it at the same time. We looked at each other and she winked.

"See you later gorgeous," Dough said, and pulled me into his embrace. His kiss left me breathless.

"See you later." I watched as he got in his car and drove away.

Samantha came to me and hugged me. "I'll bring your clothes back later in the week. See you soon."

"No hurry. I'll call you. We'll meet for lunch or something."

"Or something…" She left that hanging in the air like the beautiful rainbow.

Koshiol segues from Music to Author in her First *'release'* withBWP

2 Strippers
and a
Lesbian

Lesbian Romance
Ignites Spontaneous
All Female Threesome

SAMANTHA
KOSHIOL

Two Strippers and a Lesbian

Samantha Koshiol

One body.
Two bodies.
Three bodies.
More?
When does it become too much?

Six breasts. Six nipples. Six hands to feel 'em. Six legs. Six feet. Six ankles to be held high in the air. Six eyes. Six ears. Three different voices with three different moans. Six ears to hear them. Thirty fingers to trace the lines of the three bodies. One needs to breathe, so the two continue exhausting each other. One needs water, so the other two keep working up a sweat. One has the stamina for all three, so no minute goes wasted. All intertwined as one now, this is definitely not too much. When it comes to women, there can always be more. But the three of us at once, was more than enough.

The first time I'd had the chance to be with two women at the same time initially felt daunting. Like taking the SAT's again, I went into the room educated, yet with the possibility of a complete failure. No matter how much studying, how many prior placement tests, be it solo, or one-on-one, this was the one that counted. This was the shot at the big leagues that most people dream about. I'd made it, and was determined to make it count.

These two women were well known in my town though. They didn't necessarily have the best of reputations given their opiate addictions and rap sheets. They were still a couple of the best looking dancers at this seedy strip club on the outskirts of Northeast Minneapolis.

The club charged no cover, which was smart, because I doubt anyone would have paid to be there. They never cleaned the bathrooms. The beer taps had likely never been sanitized, but it was cheap. They chose to leave bullet holes in the wall, a decorative reminder that getting out of hand here would not be tolerated. The bouncers blocked the doors, but you could tell, even they didn't feel safe here. These ladies didn't seem to mind. A job was a job to them. Plus, they could shake it well enough that they walked out with a few hundred every night, regardless of what the house was charging them to work.

They made more money behind the scenes than on the stage, and their bosses didn't get a cut of any of that cash. That was pure profit. They weren't selling sex. They weren't selling drugs. Well, maybe some of them were, but that's not where the real money came from, for them. They were selling stories.

It may seem like high school gossip, but the middle-aged men who frequented, would pay the most to hear which of their peers were impotent. Who was a five second man? Who went home and laid hands on their wives, or girlfriends, or children? Which one couldn't wake up without a stiff Vodka-tonic? Most importantly, they wanted to know who was the biggest rock star in bed? Call it whatever you want to call it, but all it did was fuel the egos of the men. Just another good ol' pissing contest. They all wanted that number one spot, or to know who had it.

The so-called "rock stars" didn't always receive the most attention from the dancers, because, of course, that was reserved for whoever sat at the stage with the biggest wad of cash. Though they did, always get their drinks comped, and often got the closest thing to VIP this hole in the wall had to offer. Usually, that meant the quickest table service and free lap dances, as long as you still tipped after.

Strip clubs aren't in the business of giving freebies, but they will indeed bend over backward for you if you can make their dancers cum like a fire-hose.

After learning there was this favoritism, my broke ass wanted in.

My roommate, Pete and I had been coming to this place for weeks, and even though we didn't spend hundreds every time, the women seemed mighty keen on us. We started going there because I had dated one of the dancers' sister, and we were supporting her while she was earning tips to save for a honeymoon in Costa Rica. Word must have got out from the sister about my skills in the sack, based on the way we were treated. We aren't the most attractive of people, so that's the only thing that seemed to make any sense.

The second time we went to the club, this gorgeous, exotic looking, dark-toned, hazel-eyed, dancer that went by the stage name "Diamond", physically removed the hat off my head. She literally fucked herself with the bill of it, right there on stage, for everyone to see!

Never before had a woman done such a thing to me.

They usually only took my hat off to wear it themselves, like some bizarre form of staking their claim and marking their territory. The only other times I allowed them to remove my hat, was when the rest of the clothing was going to be removed along with it.

I was in shock. In awe. Confused. Horny. Disgusted. Targeted. Flattered. Albeit, also very concerned I'd be carrying some new form of STD home on my head. The over-riding feeling was without a doubt pure intrigue, though.

Did she do this to everyone wearing a hat that was sitting on "sniffers row"?

Was it something about me that she just couldn't help herself?

Maybe hats just really turned her on?

After that night, I let it go, washed the hat, just to be safe, and moved on from the whole experience. Thought I'd write it off as another strange event in my early twenties that was sparked by a woman. Another experience I'd assumed my father had likely also dealt with, since my stories started to mirror his, and I found myself walking in the same shoes, constantly. He assured me he never had such a thing happen, and had never even seen it happen to his friends. The whole thing seemed so meaningful yet pointless, so I put it in the past where it belonged.

Oddly enough, everything came full-circle

The First Time

when Diamond came into where I worked a few months later to purchase a couple hats; One for her, and one for her boyfriend. She clearly remembered me. We caught eyes when she walked in, and she began to blush.

She must have just had a thing for hats. Case closed. Right?

Diamond stayed around for ten minutes, waiting for me to customize her hats with their anniversary date. In my affair driven mind, I saw my window open, and prepared to jump. We talked to kill the time, and she asked why I hadn't been to the strip-club recently. Really, I had no real answer for her other than my lack of funds, but of course, you can't admit that to a lady. Especially one who's paying her rent, and feeding her family off of your hard earned dollars.

At this point, it'd been weeks since I had a pair of tits in my face, and I was starting to forget what an actual lap dance felt like. I sure missed both. I was positive Pete did too. Diamond told me she was working every night of the upcoming weekend, and it just so happened I was getting paid Friday. Rent had been paid for the month, and I had a little extra to blow, so this news couldn't have come at a better time.

I told her I'd be in on Sunday. God's day. Soon to be Diamonds day. She said she'd see me then. Before she left the store, she left her phone number, and hinted that I leave my schedule open that Sunday around Midnight, when the club closed.

That weekend went on, boring and uneventful like usual. Then the day came. It was Sunday.

Pete and I headed out, on towards the future, with less than $40 each, and a dream. Once we parked the car, and hit the doors of the club, I was overcome with anxiety, worried we were there for nothing but to spend our money. I felt a little reassurance when I remembered, they know we didn't have much. No, I was there for one reason: Diamond.

The plan was to fuck her in the parking lot, right after closing, in my car. Just get it done with. Cross it off the bucket list. Move on to the next one.

We bought our usual two pitchers of beer from the regular bartender. He'd grown a pretty gnarly beard since the last time we were in, another reminder of how long it had been. Going along with the familiar motions, we took a seat in front of the stage, awaiting the haphazard dancing with a fist-full of ones.

The lineup of girls was absurdly long for a Sunday night.

Pete and I sat through three, sub-par at best, dancers; my exes sister, who was arguably a much better dancer than those first three; a painfully awkward, clog-clad, woman with mismatched

The First Time

spaghetti-strap tan lines, who wouldn't know what sexy was if it were written on a hundred dollar bill and stuffed into her G-string. All of this before we saw Diamond. I tried to save my singles for her, but you can't sit at the stage, and not tip a lady for taking her clothes off.

Finally, it was her turn. The Ying Yang Twins song, "*Salt Shaker*" began, and out she walked.

Her face lit up brightly as she sauntered her way down the stage like a sex-driven runway model on the prowl. Once she reached us, she climbed that pole with glee. From the top, she removed hers. As she let it drift off by the wayside, she dropped down so hard that her ass sounded like it was on the receiving end of a hardcore paddling session. The g-force from the drop shook the entire building and the vibrations shot a dose of adrenaline into my bloodstream.

The entire time, she maintained eye contact.

When she slinked over on all fours to pick up some dollars, neatly piled into a pyramid, placed in front of us, she shoved my face between her two massive breasts. Her cleavage smelled like a sweet mixture of rose petal scented body spray, sweat and dirty money.

Diamond leaned in further and whispered, "Glad you made it, can't wait for tonight. I'm gonna show you something that you've never seen before."

After she pulled away, I was aroused and my

face was covered in glitter. My hopes to fuck her had more than been confirmed now. She wanted it just as bad as I did.

Little did I know, she had been discussing me with the other dancers for a while. They all knew of the "hat incident". I would later find out from Glo, my exes sister. It was the recent talk of the club. Diamond was a veteran there, and she found me sexy. She had no qualms telling the rest of the girls.

No wonder we had received so much attention that evening, despite our absence and our low-tax bracket scale wallets that were near empty.

Last call rang, and we guzzled the last of our stale Pabst Blue Ribbon, straight from the pitcher. Pete had been set up with another dancer, Mary, the awkward one in the clogs, for a ride home. We had planned on calling him a cab, but this ride was free. He was on his way home to his girl, so I figured that Mary's car was the only thing he'd be riding that night. I promised to be home sometime near sunrise with a great story to tell.

Soon he was on his way home, and I was on my way to a virtual stranger's, section 8 apartment, in an even dingier part of Northeast Minneapolis than the club.

Before the journey to Diamond's apartment, we met in the parking lot. I waited for her to finish paying her fees, and saying her goodnights to the other dancers. When she walked out hand-in-hand with Tia, another dancer that evening, I grew worried, assuming that this, actually had nothing to do with sex.

Tia was a known drug user and dealer. Word around town was, she sold the purest of cocaine to the higher-ups in local gangs, who then turned it into crack. They cut it with everything from baking soda to baby laxatives in order to maximize their product. Both Tia, and whoever was purchasing and manufacturing the stuff, were making a killing with the profit margins.

She was one of the few that didn't strip for the money – she made much more on the side with her cartel connections. Instead, she did it for tax purposes. She did it so she had a real income on paper; it helped to keep the police off of her tail. Tia could afford ritzy things like a BMW, Channel sunglasses, Coach bags, and even to send her kids to an upscale daycare in one of the nicest suburbs around. They'd be ostracized based on race, but so long as they got the best education there was, Tia was content. She would write off the liquid drug cash as tips from a busy night at the club, and the feds would never catch on.

A lot of women 'dance their way through college', but it was more than evident that Tia didn't need any kind of degree, or higher education, to be successful. She was smart and had her plan. It was working for her.

Tia and Diamond approached me in this parking lot, and I felt my chest get tight. I hadn't touched anything harder than pot for a few years. I was concerned that they would want me to do a few bumps or lines, at best, maybe to smoke some crack, at worst.

For most people, especially the ones with the party animal gene, doing cocaine with or off of a stripper would be a dream come true. I however, was a reformed addict who had shifted the focus onto women instead of drugs. Even while being fully aware that the possibility of a relapse was upon me, I had decided it was still worth waiting around to see what they had actually wanted from this night.

Diamond had been alluring and mysterious with her invitation. She never laid out the details. It was attractive how coy she played it, so I didn't mind the lack of further explanation when she initially asked to spend some time together. With the addictive thinking process in full-swing, the drugs didn't matter, so long as I had at least one of the women.

When they hopped into Tia's illegally funded BMW, I followed like a lost puppy.

Pulling out of the parking lot I immediately heard the flick of a lighter and suddenly the car filled with smoke and the aroma of extremely potent marijuana. Two puffs from Diamonds precious, puckered, collagen enhanced lips, and it was passed back to me.

I was hesitant to inhale, who knew what these girls were really up to.

I was already a pretty non-trusting person, and I was already allowing these two shady-seeming strangers more control than I was comfortable with. I simply didn't want to wind up drugged, robbed, and left for dead in a rough part of town. Actually, I didn't want that happening anywhere, I was sure someone would do something weird with my corpse here.

Then again, I remembered my lack of money, and their knowledge of it. Maybe they were just trying to put me at ease all along. I took a long draw, inhaled and exhaled in a relaxing manner, and passed it back up front. Finally, I was getting comfortable with whatever this experience had in store for the now three of us.

The black BMW crept slowly down the back roads and every time it's speed decreased, my pulse began to race race, yet again. After many twists and turns that seemed unnecessary to get to our destination, we made a dead stop.

We had made it to Diamonds apartment.

The complex was a mess. Absolutely run-down. There was actually a pair of brand-new shoes hanging off of the telephone line. Expensive ones. Where windows once sat, thin particle board took their place. The wood had been so carelessly scribbled on, overlapped by tags containing misspelled slurs and gang references, that you couldn't make any sense of it. Unsure of whose "turf" this was, I questioned if it were a wise choice to wear red that night. It would be my luck that this place was "owned" by an opposing gang, and I'd look like someone infiltrating from a rival.

A Lexus pulled in and before even putting the car in park, whoever was driving killed the headlights. I was pretty shaken, thinking that indeed this was a set-up. A robbery. A mugging. Whatever you want to call it. I felt like I was about to meet my maker.

Then the door of the Lexus opened. Out came a sickly skinny guy, with multiple names tattooed on his neck, wearing an XXL red-tall-tee. (thank god, I had made the right color choice) He walked straight to Tia. He pulled out a wad of Twenties so thick that the rubber band around them appeared to be stretching thin enough to snap. Suddenly, I knew we were safe. At least with this guy.

Diamond invited the three of us in behind her. The party of three that quickly turned into a party of four, and now I was close to positive there would be no sex after all. At least, I wouldn't do it with a man involved. I outgrew them as a teenager.

She closed the door behind us and as soon as it shut, Tia reached into her bra, and handed this dude a big bag filled with a white powdery substance. They did some symbolic handshake, and he was on his way.

One mystery solved, that was just a drug deal. Now left to be seen was what us three ladies were doing together here. The notion of sex returned.

As the man walked out, Diamond was up behind him just as fast to lock the deadbolt, ensuring privacy for whatever they had planned. I was just along for the ride. Clueless, I was so ready and willing to see where this would take us.

We all sat within inches of each other on one giant sofa in the living room, despite there being plenty of other seats available. Tia lit another giant, finger sized joint. At this point, I had no clue where she kept pulling them from, seeing as they were pre-rolled, but I didn't care. Diamond turned on some music as we smoked through the herb, wrapped in a zig-zag. Tia grabbed a bottle of tequila and three shot glasses, evidence that this was turning into a party.

Four shots in and they began to get up and dance with each other. Diamonds stain filled, ash-embedded throw-rug had just been turned into a stage for these two to practice their dance moves. I was sitting back watching, becoming the judge of how well they were doing.

The dancing grew more provocative, soon there was more skin exposed than there was in the club that night.

Still I sat there watching, mesmerized.

People will gladly pay for a show far less intimate than this, and here I was, in private, eyes glazed over... Watching.... For free.

As soon as they had stripped down to nothing but their panties, I became a part of the show. They each grabbed one of my hands, and pulled me off of the couch.

Up I followed, letting their hands guide me. I found myself sandwiched between these two scantily clad dancers. Diamond and Tia grabbed each other's shoulders, with me still between them, and started moving slowly with the pulse of the music.

Seductively, they moved up and down slowly on my stiff, awkward body like a pole, swaying to a particularly lusty Al Green song the entire time. They didn't miss a beat.

Of course, they had been formally trained to do this.

I kept that locked in the back of my mind while trying to maintain my cool. I was just along for the ride, and they were taking turns driving. Diamond was in the driver's seat, as she was situated in front of me. She shifted her hold from Tia's shoulders to my jaw-line.

Diamond pulled me in. Face to face. Lips to lips. She released pent up passion through a meaningful kiss.

There were zero questions about the experience now. I was getting more than just a dose of Diamond, Tia was the package deal. How exactly was this happening? Fuck it, I was just happy that it was.

The pressure of pleasuring not one, but two strippers grew insurmountable.

This was a first for me, and though I was incredibly confident of my skills in the art of multiple orgasms, it had only ever been with one woman at a time. Traveling this road was something I always thought that I would be comfortable with, but knowing my actions could suffer from performance anxiety, with these two particular women, was just about enough to cause it. Lord knows that would be this week's hot topic if it happened like that.

This was a challenge. Maybe it was a test. It was without a doubt, the holy grail of sexual conquests, and I needed to make sure the opportunity didn't pass by half-assed. I needed to seize the day! Carpe Diem and that booty! I had to make my ancestors proud, seeing as they had been the ones to pass down the perversion laden lifestyle to me through the gene pool. Who knows if any of them had a chance like this?

So now, facing what destiny had mapped out, with a real sense of clarity, I was ready. There really wasn't much of a choice. Especially if I wanted to maintain my reputation for being the bearer of orgasms.

I took the wheel and started driving. Pedal to the metal. I accelerated quickly into the dark with no headlights, blind to whatever was ahead of me. I figured I'd floor it, and either crash or beat the previous racers record. There was no point in being careful, no point in being steady. That would only end on some inadequate, stuck in the middle, point. That would leave me left in the dust with the many men (probably some other women, also) that had traveled the same paths behind this same wheel.

That passionate kiss from Diamond lead to hands exploring bodies. First, Diamonds roaming mine. Releasing my face from her soft grasp, her hands were now free to explore further. They moved down the curves of my shoulders, teasing her own finger along the way. They reached the small of my back as I held back an excitement filled shudder, and she pulled me in again. Closer. Tighter. She was breathing near my ear calmly and calculated. Her lips moved while letting out a tiny noise that hinted at desire, and she placed them on my neck.

Tia approached her from behind, grabbing Diamonds waist and using it as a guide up her side, trailing all the way to breasts. Reading Diamonds reaction, I followed along. Tia was caressing the shape of them. Reading them like two crystal balls. I poignantly stroked her nipples with my fingertips.

Her nipples were like a flip that switched, and turned her on full arousal mode.

She pushed her weight, all the while pulling Tia along, against my torso with anticipation. We all toppled backward onto the couch behind me. That was the couch of destiny. The couch where I once sat, so confused as to what was happening. The couch that I was now entering a full-on threesome with two strippers on. The couch that would be my launching pad to success among local strangers. The couch that was meant to turn an average retail employee into an overnight sexual celebrity with their very own 15 minutes of fame.

The three of us lasted on that couch for much longer than 15 minutes, as my primary rule of thumb remained intact: don't ever, ever, dare leave a woman with less than three orgasms. That's just common courtesy. If she's gonna take the time to get naked, let you touch her, and give you the chance to make her moan, you better at least attempt to leave her with no less than three orgasms. They all deserve it, and most men have trouble living up to the three orgasm minimum. This usually ensures that ladies have at least one as a token of appreciation. If you can't do that, just don't have sex. You're wasting their precious time.

In total, this round, there were 11. Four on Tia's part, six on Diamonds behalf, and one extremely worthwhile, draining one of my own.

The first was Diamond. It happened so quickly, I thought she was faking it. Anticipation had just been getting to her, that much.

Tia was still playing with Diamonds nipples, which were now harder than ice caps covering mountains left uncharted. While she was toying with her apparent arousal center, Tia situated the lower half of her body, calculatedly, onto Diamonds face. I was busy down below, starting to part her lips with my fingers, when I felt it happen.

She came so hard that I was worried that there'd be water damage to her couch. It was pretty obvious that she hadn't felt the touch of a woman in an extremely long time. I was happy to be that woman and more than positive that Tia agreed.

Diamond wasn't ready to switch things up yet. She grabbed my hand by the fingers and placed them upon her soaking wet, pulsating clitoris, begging me to continue. I obliged, following whatever she desired.

The First Time

Tia sat perfectly positioned on Diamonds jaw-line and as I remained on keeping her clitoris stimulated, she started tracing Tia's with her tongue. This caused Tia to forcefully squeeze Diamonds nipples that she still had hold of. She kept squeezing tighter and tighter as Diamonds tongue went faster and faster.

While this was happening, I found myself in a dumbstruck awe, unbelieving that this was seriously what my Sunday night had turned into.

I snapped back into it when I felt Tia's leg give-way and shake as she started to have her first orgasm. Simultaneously, Diamond clenched the couch cushions, and soon I felt another wave of wetness come soaking down my hand.

Knowing how sensitive she still was, I proceeded to switch my fingers out with my tongue. Swirling it around the scope of her clitoris, and teasing her by pulling away every time she started to arch her back. Tia was still planted on Diamonds face, only her hands had shifted to Diamonds hair, pulling it loosely like a riding crop. I reached up and started playing with her nipples to see if she liked it as much as Diamond had. She did.

Within a matter of minutes, they both came again, one after another, like a perverted game of dominoes.

I stayed focused. Continuing on with my tongue on Diamond, I lifted one hand from Tia's voluptuous breasts and went for Diamonds g-spot. One finger. Two fingers. Three fingers and she began moaning and pushing back, like she was holding off yet another orgasm. Quickly I put one more finger in, just to test the waters, and she was done for. She let it out like it was the first orgasm she had in months, even though this was already her fourth of the night.

Sensing they needed a break, I pulled away.

Diamond clenched her thighs tightly around my head and pulled me back. She wasn't ready for a break yet. This woman was relentless!

Tia was ready for a change of pace, and she removed herself from Diamonds face to situate herself on the other side of me on the couch. Diamond was far too distracted by my clitoral manipulation, she was leaving Tia high and dry. Tia was also becoming jealous of all the attention Diamond was receiving.

So now, these two naked women laid, one on either side of me. Their knees facing the ceiling, legs spread open in anticipation. Waiting.

I decided that Diamond had her fair share of my tongue and it was Tia's turn. I kept my right hand with Diamond, tweaking her nipples until my hand found its way back down below, back to her g-spot. Three fingers kept applying pressure, and I let it build slower this time. My left hand was doing the same to Tia, only my thumb and tongue were taking turns working her clitoris while the rest of my fingers were working their way along her g-spot. It all began escalating, fast.

Tia was pulling at my hair this time. An indication from her that I was doing an excellent job. Diamond didn't seem to mind that my attention was focused on Tia, as she was still twitching in a way that said she was ready to have another orgasm at any time.

Soon it happened. Both came like they were racing each other to the finish line, and they were both winners.

The race still wasn't over. They were going to make sure I got mine also. We stayed in the same position, as I wasn't done with them yet either. They both reached over in my direction. Completely ignoring any nipple play, their hands met below my waistline. With how smoothly they did this, they either must have done it before, or agreed on their actions beforehand.

Diamond's choice: the clitoris. Tia's choice: g-spot.

We intertwined like some sort of nude, breast and leg, entangled pretzel, with arms bent over each other, all headed towards one primary goal. After a few minutes of work, I could sense they were both ready. I was sure as fuck ready. Watching these two get off so many times had me on edge. The whole time I was trying to hold back because it was almost always one and done for me. One of the few things I had in common with most men. Any more than one would have personally killed my stamina. The fact that I had saved it for both of their final orgasms created this buildup of pressure and pleasure, that led to screams and uncontrollable thrashing so loud that Diamonds neighbors ended up calling the police.

Thankfully, we had already finished by the time they arrived. The two male officers seemed rather impressed when they came to survey the situation. The stouter of the two, the one that looked like he was failing at growing out his facial hair, even asked me for some tips.

There weren't really any tips to give. You either understand how a woman's body works or you don't. The fact that I share the same parts as them probably gives me an unfair advantage, though.

He shook his head in an earnest fashion that explained he had been told that before. He also gave me a 'congrats' on conquering the ever long quest most men dream about. I must have still been riding high on the flow of estrogen because the toothy grin on my face wasn't fading.

The two officers got in their car and drove off. They left behind a new-found piece of pride for me. Cops and I didn't generally see eye to eye, but they had an initial respect for me, based on the fact they knew I could probably please their wives better than they could.

Early that morning, I went home a changed woman. I had planned to tell Pete the details, but I was now uncaring as to who knew and who didn't. I was proud of myself for accomplishing the unthinkable. This was my notch, no one else's.

Still, every time a middle aged man walked into that hat store, over the course of the following month, and gave me an acknowledging wink, I was reassured. The girls were talking about me, and sharing the story of their new favorite rock star.

We hope you enjoyed these 5 stories.

But wait... there's more!

You are correct. There are still many pages left to read. We love to give our readers a bonus at the end of each collection. So, rather than just 5 stories, you just got 6!

Introducing our newest author, a crazy ol' coot, Mr. Cody Beltow.

Enjoy!

89 YEAR OLD AUTHOR
TELLS TALES SIMILAR TO
OTHERS IN EROTICA GENRE

MY UNCLE'S GIRLFRIEND

Virgin has Threesome at the Whitehouse Motel

CODY BELTOW

Bonus
My Uncle's Girlfriend
Cody Beltow

My uncle was a man that didn't put up with any shit. He was an iron worker. He was also instrumental in me getting my first piece of ass.

There was none of that incest crap, mind you. My uncle loved me in his brutish kind of way. He helped raise me, so to speak. Helped me become a man, and he didn't want me to go into the world after high school as a virgin, so he arranged for me to fuck his girl.

Well…we both fucked her really. I guess you could classify it as a threesome.

The First Time

It seemed to me back then, everyone was having sex. My Grandad was definitely okay with it, he had his collection of girlie mags in the back pocket of his Lazyboy in the basement. He wasn't ashamed of them or anything, quite the opposite of my mother and stepdad. I spent almost every minute at Grandad's house down in the basement with those lovely ladies. I wonder if my Grandad left them there on purpose, knowing I needed the release.

He had them all, Cherry, Hustler, IOU you know the ones that show it all, intercourse and even had some good stories from time to time. Other than comic books, that was about the extent of reading for me. There was always at least two or three in the pocket in the back of his recliner. As soon as I arrived, I would go down and pop on the TV and grab his mags. Everyone else was upstairs shootin' the shit and I guess they just thought I was watching TV. As long as I can remember, and as long as he was alive, you could find me down there beatin' my meat to one of his centerfold hotties.

Then there was my best friend, Kip. His dad had big trash bags full of every issue of Playboy, Penthouse, Hustler and a few of my fav's IOU and Cherry. You know, the big 50 gallon trash bags. Can you imagine 50 gallons of porn? I can tell you, from what Kip and I used to see in those beautiful glossy black plastic receptacles…every time I see one today I have a flashback that brings a smile to my face. I love black plastic bags…or at least what they kept private inside. Funny, it's a smaller version today, buy a product from an adult store and they give you a black bag to carry it home in.

Kip's dad used to store them up in the attic. There were seven bags full, heck probably more. A teenage boys wet dream, literally. We spent a lot of hot attic time over the years. That was until his mom discovered what was going on with us being up there so much. She had them moved. It wasn't long though until Kip came running into my back yard shortly after to whisper in my ear he had found them. Apparently his dad had won out and his mom had not been allowed to throw them away. They had simply been moved to the cellar. I was back in my element again. It's not like we were doing circle jerks. Heck, that would have constituted one of us being gay. Couldn't have that in our little town, people talk about bullying now. You'd just get your ass kicked until you moved out of town. It wasn't considered bullying back then, it was just growing up straight.

Kip and I did have competitions though.

The First Time

We sometimes raced to see who could cum first, and other times we battled it out to see who could maintain a high speed without cumming. I thought it all pretty normal. Everyone at school said they had already had sex by the time we were juniors. In the barely 18 and over category, I was supposedly the only real virgin left in the county. I'm not sure I believe it, it's just what they all said. Not that it was a big school, or a big town either. Just 23 kids in my graduating class, 135 total in the entire school, and I believe at that time the town held just light of 1500.

***

I almost went all the way when I was younger. I had a girlfriend for a short while. I was very proud of that. Every guy would give me the elbows on Friday and ask if this was the weekend. I smiled and went on my way.

Sure, she was a knockout. I definitely wanted to fuck her, I just wasn't brought up that way. My parents, mom, and step-dad had brought me up on the religious side of the tracks. In fact, they used to scorn it all. Sex, Drugs, & Rock n Roll. I wasn't allowed to listen to it, I was told to never do it or her. I was told if I did drugs I would die. I was told I had to wait till I was married, and I was told the music was the gateway to all evil. We actually do tend to side with what our parents tell us when we are young, at least to a point.

Sarah and I had gotten to third base, although I was always the well trained gentleman, and kept us from going all the way.

I remember this one time though. It was the most difficult date I ever had, in the restraining part that is. We almost went there. If it hadn't been for the asshole in the car next to us, we would have.

I picked Sarah up that night and she was looking especially beautiful in her (need the correct kind of clothes here). When I look back today, I think she was actually trying to tip the balance. She wanted to do it, even more than I did.

I took her to our pop stand. We got a soda and sat on the hood for a while, chatting with all the other kids. Then everyone headed out. It was 'that time'.

We all made our way up to make-out drive. Kip had snagged a couple beers from his dad and someone had hinted they had a joint. Pretty much everyone was in the habit of drinking by then. It was nothing to get any kind of alcohol for us, it was normal. Damn! The town had 3 bars and 3 liquor stores if you counted that one of them was both. Find someone of age and buy them a bottle, or six pack, you had a start to that night's party. Wow! When I think about the bottles of premixed Orange screwdriver we had gone through.

It was two weeks before we would move away. I had never smoked marijuana before. I set my mind that night, if I couldn't get my pecker wet, I was going to do something else. I had decided to try it as soon as it was mentioned.

Kip and his girl were on the right and some other kid I don't quite remember on the left. Like I said though if it weren't for that kid...well...let's just say, I would probably have one with Sarah today.

I think it was Grady who passed the joint around. It was pretty small. What I would definitely call a pinner today. Grady was smart about it. He hadn't told everyone, just a few of us. He knew it wouldn't go far.

There were six of us, Grady and his girl Rebecca, Kip, and his girl...I think he was dating Wendy at the time, I can't keep his girls straight though, and me and Sarah. We each got two hits. Grady about burnt his fingers on the last toke and that was it.

We all stood in our tight little circle starin' at each other, waitin'. Then Wendy giggled. It was a cute little giggle, just two bubbles. That was all it took though. The rest of us burst out and the circle expanded like a flower. Each of us like a puffy umbrella from those dandelion weeds, blowing on the wind.

Bonus My Uncle's Girlfriend

All the other folks started to get suspicious after a while, or maybe it was paranoia. Most of us had been drinking, especially after the joint, yet we were all the hit of the party.

Sarah finally convinced me we should get in the back seat. I knew the drill. She loved to make out, and up on the hill, she was apt to grab my pecker and give it a few jerks for me. I was up for it of course.

She had these great perky tits, full and round, with tiny pink nipples. After I had got her shirt and bra off, I dove in. I can still remember how her body tensed up whenever I would roll her nubs between my teeth. Just lightly, not to hurt.

I reached down between her legs, up her skirt. I was surprised to find no panties this time. I looked up at her and she gave me a sheepish grin.

"Always prepared," she said to me as she lifted her knees and her skirt rolled up to her waist.

Man! I was in a new state of mind, totally high, and here was my hottie, open and ready for penetration, with only my jeans and underwear as a barrier. Thoughts of keeping her a 'good girl' were nowhere to be found.

My fingers slid into her juicy crevice as she unbuttoned my pants. The big man in charge down there was beatin' at the door to get out. She continued with the zipper as I pushed my fingers in and out of her, picking up speed. She moaned, kissed me, and told me I was doing it right. I was thankful for that.

You know when you are hot and heavy, and then she grabs your dick? Especially when you are younger… It kinda takes your breath away.

Her hand was so hot. She moved my clothes out of the way. She's pumping it slowly, although, at the same time, she's kinda guiding it toward her pussy. She pulled me on top of her and pointed the way with my dick. I was right there, then damn it all, that cock-sucker had to interrupt us.

I guess they had gotten in some kind of fight. They had gotten out of the car and she shoved him onto the side of my car. It caused the car to rock and that got my attention. I think the paranoid thing was still kickin' from the weed too, and I got all nervous that we were getting in trouble.

I whipped my pants back up and threw her shirt over her before getting out of the car to find out what was going on. I was pissed when I found out it was just a squabble from the riffraff. In retrospect, it was the best thing that ever happened to me.

I got my wits about me again and took Sarah home shortly after that. She was pretty quiet on the way home and broke up with me a few days later. Everyone at school thought we parted because we did do it, when it was actually because we didn't. No matter. We moved a few towns away and I never saw her again. I did hear through the weeds, she had gotten pregnant just six months later. She hadn't even made it to senior.

Friends told friends, and I was awarded the status of 'having done it' at my new school. I didn't correct anyone. I thought I had gotten close enough to the act to keep from saying anything stupid. My upbringing helped as I became one who didn't fuck-and-tell.

***

There I was, with the whole school believing I was part of the pack, my senior year, when my Uncle asked me.

We were riding in his big conversion van. He had it all tricked out with a bed in the back. On this particular day though, the bed was folded into a couch. He was carrying some stuff back there, and we couldn't get to the bed anyway.

The radio was blaring some music. Can't say as I remember what we were listening to, although he was definitely the coolest to hang out with, so I know it was something I liked. We had a lot of similarities, including our taste in music. Of course, he had been the one to introduce me to any music I had ever heard, so I didn't really have an opinion. I listened to what he listened to, and I liked it.

The First Time

He had taken me to the titty bar where his girlfriend worked on this day. She was done with her shift soon. Another perk of having him as my relation. He let me do some stuff, things that would have my parents rolling in their graves if they knew.

You see, I was raised by what you might call, freaks. They were the true, out in left fielders. I didn't know it back then, I do now. My parents were extremely religious. They said music lead to the Devil, so the only time I got to listen to it was when I was with my uncle. I told you I had done some drinkin'. What I didn't tell you, my dad was a cop. He had me so brainwashed about drinking that I was always the designated driver. He said I would go to Hell if I got to drinkin' too much. Plus, he was heavy handed with his belt. He would take to beatin' my back side to bruises, sometimes for no apparent reason. I knew, if he ever caught wind that I was drinking, let's just say, I might not walk straight for a while.

That would be why my uncle took it upon himself to see that I had…experiences. Things a boy from an ordinary family would get to do and see. He knew about the porn magazines, so he knew I would be into girls. He also knew I was pretty shy around the women. I think that is why he took me to his hangouts so often. He was trying to get me used to them.

Bonus My Uncle's Girlfriend

I took my lead from him wherever we went. He had an air about him, that 'don't fuck with me' air. Most people listened to the air's advice. It didn't hurt that he was built like a linebacker.

We walked into the strip club and sat at the stage like it was no big deal that I was a kid. The bouncer came over when he noticed us and tried to kick me out. My uncle wouldn't have it though. He told him to go fuck off. He informed the bouncer that it didn't matter because I wasn't drinking and his girlfriend was about to go on stage. Once she was finished with her set, we would all be on our way, so the bouncer needed to go mind his own fucking business.

My uncle had stood up during his pseudo instructions, maybe the bouncer decided it wasn't worth it since he stood a good head shorter than my Uncle. Probably a good 50 pounds of muscle shy to boot. As I said, he got to do pretty much whatever he wanted most of the time. I know I would never dream of going up against a man like him.

So, there I was, watching the girl's parade by. It wasn't anything like some of the clubs I've been in today. I don't think clubs were allowed to go nude back then. They had bottoms and pasties, nothing really showing. I always wonder why we men are so into giving up the dough to see a woman in a bikini, when we can just go to the beach for free. I guess it's the attention. Them makin' you feel like they are there for you. Plus, at the beach, the girls are running around in the water, they aren't up in your face, close enough to lick 'em.

We passed our share of bills out accordingly and when his girl was finished with her set, he and I went out to the van to wait for her. He had been drilling me on what I had seen in there, asking me what I thought about the girls if I wanted to fuck them or not. So when she gets in, the topic of conversation is all about women and sex.

I thought she was a super cool lady. I was still really nervous being around a woman though. Sarah was as close as I had ever gotten. Granted, that was pretty close, although she was the only one. Plus, she was my age. Women…you know, mature women…they were out of my range back then.

I was bumbling all over my words every time she asked me something. We were in these big captain's chairs, hers turned to the back facing me. It was cozy, yet uncomfortable at the same time. I wasn't used to a woman talking to me, let alone about sex and the ways of the world.

Finally, he must have started to suspect. My uncle asked me if I had had sex. I could have shriveled into a fly at that moment. I denied it at first. They kept on though, and I finally confessed.

My uncle got irate. He starts cussin', accusing

people (my parents) of not teaching a boy correctly. Then he turns to me, "What the fuck! Why didn't you tell me you were a virgin?"

I didn't know if I was in trouble, or what. I knew all the kids at school would laugh, I didn't want my favorite relative to laugh. I nodded my head in shame.

He turns to his girl and says, "Well, baby… You can help him with that, can't you?"

She was like, "What? Really? Are you sure about that?"

I didn't need to hear or even see him to know what his answer would be. He said what he said because he always meant it. He never bullshitted. He said as much, "I wouldn't have asked you if I wasn't sure, now would I?"

Surprisingly, she said, "Well, sure. Yes, I'll do whatever you want me to babe."

I think it was the first motel we came to after she agreed. One minute we're driving down the road and literally the next, swerve, he swings in. It was called the White House. I remember it clearly. It was still there the last time I visited. He told us to stay in the van as he was telling them he was only getting the room for him and her.

We get in the room and my uncle brought in half a liquor bar with him. We're drinkin' beer and wine, they get all naked and start kissin'. Finally, all shy and bashful, I start to get out of my clothes. They had already made it to full on fucking by then. It took me quite a while due to being that nervous. I was damn near shaking in my non-existent boots.

If I hadn't been so damn nervous, I'm sure I would have had a raging hard on from the get go, watching them fuck. I would get chub and then my nerves would kill it. Back and forth my dick was not listening, all the while, they're bangin' away.

I did manage to get completely naked finally, and get onto the bed with them. They were at a good clip by this time, he's pounding away. I'm just watching in amazement, him with his big ol' long cock, fucking her pussy. This is the first time I'm actually getting to have somewhat of a good look at one. She's moanin' and groanin'. Then she starts touchin' on me. I'm surprised I didn't just piss myself right there.

You know that first time, when your body starts shakin'. I'm just there, all nervous, not able to do much of anything with my 'mister limpy.'

They finish. Both of them had orgasms and my uncle lays down on the other side of her. I didn't know what to do. I'm just lying there. They're talking, having another drink, smoking cigarettes. He tells her how great it was and I'm thinking to myself, oh my god!

My uncle finally said to me, "Well, boy... Aren't you gonna get up and fuck that thing?

That's what you're here for."

I still can't get my damn cock to obey though. So he tells her, and she does it. She rolls over and starts giving me a blow job. She's rubbin' her tits on my dick, gettin' it good and hard. She tells me to get on top, so I get on top to get down to business.

Keep in mind, I was still a squirrely son of a bitch. When I went into the military, I only weighed in at 138 and still an inch shorter than I am today. She wasn't huge, but she was still a lot bigger than me.

So I get on that. I can still remember, that pussy was all wet, his jizz and hers. I still was so clueless, it still took me a while to figure out what I was doing, till I finally got it in. I wasn't super attracted to her or anything, she wasn't some rockin' model, this was backwoods stripper club material. She definitely had a rockin' body though, no doubt about that.

I went to poundin' it, and just kept poundin', and poundin'. About that time, the nervous shit hit me again and I lost my hard on. She goes to givin' me head again, gets me at attention. I pounded her some more until my Uncle decided it was his turn.

"Hey, man. Get the fuck off, it's my turn again," he chided.

He literally just pushed me off and starts

poundin' that shit again.

We get this running joke started. A lot of my relations are into wrestling. He would 'tap in' and say things like, "Good match. Next up, the heavy weight."

We'd slap hands and he would jump back in the ring. It got my nerves to take a break at least, it became a game in my head. I would jump up on the bed and bounce around before slammin' my cock home.

This goes on for hours, and hours. I remember when we finally quit, and we probably wouldn't have stopped, we would have gone on…who knows how long? I know he did a lot more fuckin' than I did. I should be damn proud of myself at how many times I came, and how many hard-ons I got that night.

It was eleven o'clock the next morning when the Indian came to the room and tried to kick us out. He knocked on the door and said it was check-out time. We were already supposed to be out.

My uncle said, "Yea, yea… We're gonna get out. Fuck off!"

The guy leaves and we go back to fuckin' his girl. Half an hour later they guy comes back and is banging on the door, "you have to get out, or I'm going to call the police."

Not a good thing to say to my uncle. "Mother fucker! I will come out there and kick your mother fuckin' ass. We'll get out of this room when we get out."

I had the girl bent over the bed, poundin' her from behind when the guy comes back a third time, claiming he was about to call the cops. My uncle said, "Time!" Another wrestling joke to call it quits.

We got dressed, I don't think we even cleaned up, we got out of the room around twelve-thirty. I believe, it is truly, the one and only time, that I still to this day can remember my cock being that sore for a good week and a half after. We fucked so much it just got rubbed raw.

A life lesson though. I took instruction from a champion of the bedroom. I have been around quite a few more situations like that in my day now. I have to say, not many men can do what my uncle could. Hell, what I can. I have had quite a few women knockin' at my door because I was the only one who could rock their world for hours on end. I'll tell you about some of those girls later…

About the Authors

V.B.Eghan

I would like to thank my readers for buying my story. Your reviews are the fuel that keeps my imagination firing. I am ever grateful to Black Widow Publishing for taking my stories from concept to finished product. The beautiful, imaginative book designs by Jennifer Fitzgerald are undeniably the best!

I have to mention my family for putting up with uncooked meals, piles of laundry, and a messy house, while I am embroiled in my writing. Without your support, and encouragement, I would never be able to finish. For that I am eternally in your debt. I love you all.

If you are a fan, or would like to catch up with what is coming next, you can contact me at my publisher's website. They have a great Reader's Club, you can get coupons for up to 50% off our books!

Connect with Vanessa

Like - Follow - Friend
Find Vanessa at all of these locations.

Vanessa's Publisher:
http://BlackWidowPublishing.com

Vanessa's Twitter Page:
https://twitter.com/VBreckEghan

Vanessa's Facebook Page:
http://on.fb.me/1DDu0GP

Vanessa's Pinterest Page:
https://www.pinterest.com/vanessa-BreckEghan

Samantha Writner

Hi, I am Samantha Writner. I grew up in the cold north of Philadelphia. As a child I swore to never live there when I got older. I have kept to my word and now roam the southern states, the islands, and even further south countries. I don't actually have a permanent home base, and with my love for travel, it suits me fine.

My favorite saying is, "Pretend to be an Extrovert, it keeps the blues away." Using this way of thinking has afforded me to meet many friends and hear many stories, some of which I will share with you.

I hope you have enjoyed my story here, *Me & My Nympho*. Please leave a review on Amazon. Then come chat with me on my publisher's website.

Check out my novel *Threesomes Cum*. It is book one of a trilogy. The second is due out in late 2015. Visit Amazon for a paperback or kindle copy of book one now.

Other stories by Samantha

http://bit.ly/3some-cum

Connect with Samantha

Like - Follow - Friend
Find Samantha at all of these locations:

Samantha's Publisher:
http://BlackWidowPublishing.com

Samantha's Facebook Page:
https://www.facebook.com/SamanthaWritner

Samantha's Twitter:
https://twitter.com/BlackWidowPress

Samantha's Goodreads:
http://bit.ly/goodreads-writner

Kat Crimson

Thank you & congratulations on making it all the way to the end! If you enjoyed *Seduced by 2*, I encourage you to show your support by leaving a review for us online, and tell a friend.

A bit about me... I'm just a creative Kat with a kinky brain and a dark and filthy-sweet imagination, looking to share my juice with the rest of the kinksters out there. I really hope you've enjoyed my erotic ramblings thus far, and will continue to share in my adventures with me. Please don't be shy with reviews – I love to get feedback from you on my work.

Thank you so much for your support!

~ Kat Crimson ^,,^

Other stories by Kat

http://bit.ly/bait-the-hook

http://bit.ly/jizziebelle

Connect with Kat

Like - Follow - Friend
Find Kat at all of these locations.

Kat's Publisher:
http://BlackWidowPublishing.com

Kat's Facebook Page:
https://www.facebook.com/KatCrimson

Kat's Wordpress Blog:
https://curi0usitykilledkat.wordpress.com/

Kat's Twitter:
https://twitter.com/katcrimson_auth

Kat on Goodreads:
http://bit.ly/goodreads-crimson

Kat at Smashwords:
http://smashwords.com/profile/view/
KatCrimson

Cassidy Phoenyx

To my readers….

I am just a shy girl with a naughty little mind that enjoys sharing my various exploits with others. I live alone in this log cabin deep in the heart of Maine. I am a chef by trade and find that it is a great creative outlet for my passions. The cold lonely nights allow my mind to wander. If you enjoy my work, please read my debut short story " The door to ecstasy."   I am forever grateful for your patronage. Thank you for coming along with me on this voyage.

A special thanks goes out to my editor Susan Allen, for her patience with me as I continue to explore my interest in writing. Thank you to black widow publishing for giving me this chance. Please leave a review at whichever forum that you have purchased my story from. Your feedback is always appreciated.

Other stories by Cassidy

http://bit.ly/door-to-ecstasy

Connect with Cassidy

Like - Follow - Friend
Find Cassidy at all of these locations.

Cassidy's Publisher:
http://BlackWidowPublishing.com

Cassidy's Goodreads:
http://bit.ly/goodreads-phoenyx

Cassidy's Twitter:
https://twitter.com/cassidyphoenyx

Cassidy's Facebook:
https://www.facebook.com/cassidy.phoenyx

Samantha Koshiol

I have been writing since I could make sense of words. I started writing books about Lego's taking over the universe as a child. As an angsty young teen, I shifted to writing prose and emotional poetry. Then when adulthood came, I started writing about my main focus: women.

Once I started writing about women, I couldn't stop. The women I dated and interacted with have left some pretty jaw-dropping, depressing, tantalizing, enigmatic, and taboo memories. The stories about them started in Minnesota, but have since expanded with my traveling (and meeting crazy women) to places like Key West, New Orleans and Denver. Keep an eye out for more stories from myself, especially my first official book: Long Legs in the Twin Cities. That will be out in the summer of 2015 through Black Widow Publishing.

A quick thanks to everyone who took the time to read my words. A longer thanks to those of you that enjoyed it. An extended thanks to any of you who enjoyed it enough that you'll leave a review and come back to read more. Finally, the biggest of thanks to the people who've supported, motivated, and pushed me to pursue a career in writing. I fucking love you guys. See you next time... and if you can't wait until then, catch up with me via social media on one (or more, or all) of the various platforms:

Connect with Samantha

Like - Follow - Friend
Find Samantha at all of these locations.

Samantha's Publisher:
http://BlackWidowPublishing.com

Samantha's Facebook:
https://www.facebook.com/
samanthakoshiolismyfavoriteauthor

Samantha's Twitter:
https://twitter.com/skosho

Samantha's Instagram:
https://instagram.com/skosho/

Samantha's Webpage:
http://longlegsinthetwincities.com/

Cody Beltow

Cody is a rockin' 89 years young. He loves to tell the tales of his life and one day, someone at Black Widow Publishing got an ear full. He had some pretty racy tales and agreed to let us publish them. We hope he will tell us a few more, as they are bound to be full of hot and spicy romance… or just straight up sex.

He said he doesn't want anything to do with social networking. Maybe if we get enough people coming to our website to ask for him, he will reconsider.

http://BlackWidowPublishing.com

www.ingramcontent.com/pod-product-compliance
Lightning Source LLC
Chambersburg PA
CBHW071254250626
47159CB00004B/1173